ALL THE WRIGHT MOVES

ALL THE WRIGHT MOVES

K.A. LINDE

PART I

ROOMMATES

1

NORA

There was absolutely no way that she just said what I thought she said.

No way.

Not in a hundred million years.

Tamara stared back at me expectantly. Maybe even hopeful. But I still could not process a word that had come out of her mouth. Let alone that she was standing in my office at Wright Vineyard at all. Certainly not for *this*.

"Nora?" she asked with a flip of her bright red hair.

I had no response.

I hadn't seen my ex–best friend in a solid ten months. And it was for the better since she'd slept with my boyfriend of three years. I'd moved out of our apartment the next day, blocked her number, and avoided her at all costs.

Now, she was here.

And hey, I loved planning weddings. I'd been doing it for years, ever since I'd interned at a prestigious company here in Lubbock during college. Now, I ran my own ship at my brother's vineyard and got to work with dozens of beautiful brides-to-be.

I'd always envisioned my own wedding. Might or might not have secretly planned the entire thing with my ex, August, while we were together. It was my *job* after all.

But I certainly hadn't considered planning *this* wedding.

My ex–best friend was standing in front of me.

Asking me to plan *her* wedding.

To *my* ex.

"Come again?" I said, blinking in confusion.

She thrust the shiny diamond in my face. "We got engaged!"

As if *that* were the part that I'd missed.

"Right," I said slowly.

"It happened yesterday, downtown at West Table. He popped the question right there at a candlelit dinner. The entire room applauded for us."

Whatever she said after that was lost to my blood pressure, which chose that moment to shoot through the roof. Blood rushed into my ears, my heart rate skyrocketed, and everything went perfectly quiet.

Except, you know, my mind.

I couldn't stop replaying every single thing that had happened in my life to reach this moment. Tamara dating August senior year of high school for a whole three months before dumping him for some football player. August and I reconnecting our junior year of college, and Tamara encouraging me to go for it. I'd had exactly zero boyfriends, and when he'd asked me out, I'd said yes. Yes, yes, yes.

Usually, guys were scared off by two things: Hollin and Campbell. My two older brothers were terrifying in their own rights. Hollin was *huge*, tatted, and drove a Harley while Campbell was literally the biggest rockstar in the world right now. Add that to the fact that when I got around guys, I turned into a shy, tongue-tied wallflower, and it had never been a good match.

Three years with August. Three *years*, and I'd been sure he was *the one*. Whatever that meant. Then last summer, I'd caught him making out with Tamara backstage at an event. Hollin had punched August in the face, I had been spirited away, and suddenly, my life was over. No boyfriend. No best friend. No apartment.

All to land me in this radioactive, boiling hell.

Tamara must have finally realized I wasn't listening. She'd never been quick on the uptake. "Nora, aren't you excited for us?" Her voice was syrupy sweet. As if she knew precisely what card she was playing here.

I hated conflict unless it was work-related.

"Um..." I shook my head and cleared my throat.

"So, will you do it? We were thinking a fall wedding here at the vineyard with lots and lots of flowers. You know how much I love fresh blooms. We always used to keep them in our apartment. Plus, August loves—"

"I'm going to stop you there," I said firmly but kindly.

Tamara's mouth dropped open slightly in surprise. She was the kind of extrovert who collected introverts to follow her around and pad her ego. She'd lost that when she betrayed me. I didn't owe her anything at this point. And certainly not the rest of this conversation.

Before I'd gotten my wedding planning gig, I'd worked at Best Buy for eight months and perfected the way to say *fuck off* with a smile and doe eyes. I was always professional. I was always perfectly nice. But I brooked no argument.

Customer service voice activate!

"As much as I appreciate you coming to the winery today to talk to us about your upcoming nuptials, we're fully booked for the fall. We couldn't even fit in one more client." I smiled at her in a *go fuck yourself* way, teetering on my signature four-inch high heels and tapping the large brown planner I used for the season.

"Well, what about next spring?" Tamara pushed.

"Oh, that would be lovely. Spring flowers and all," I said serenely. I pretended to check the schedule. "I'm afraid not."

"You *cannot* be booked through next spring."

"Oh, we're not. But unfortunately, the vineyard will be unavailable to you at that time. Anything else?"

"You can't refuse me service," Tamara snapped.

We were perfectly within our rights to say no to whoever we wanted. And I hadn't even said no. I'd smiled and looked pleasant. I might have been a wallflower with boys, but I wasn't going to be pushed around by the woman who had hurt me. Not at work, where I was in my element.

"We're certainly not refusing you service," I told her calmly. "However, you're not entitled to a wedding here, and I don't think we'd be a good fit."

"Nora, come on," Tamara said, reaching for fake tears. I knew that trick all too well. "You're my best friend. I miss you so much. I hoped this would bring us back together."

"That's lovely for you." I blinked at her and said nothing else.

Tamara's jaw set. She wanted me to say more. To feed into her ego and give her ammunition to use against me. But I'd cried enough tears at the loss of this friendship. If she had come back in those first few months when I was a broken mess, I might have even relented. Been the trampled dog she'd created all those years ago.

But I'd found out that I could survive on my own. I still missed having her around. I missed our stupid inside jokes and sleepovers and parties. That wasn't enough to fix this.

Tamara stomped her foot like a child when they didn't get their way. "Nora, how dare you! This is ridiculous! You're supposed to be providing a service."

I opened my mouth to reach for those customer service instincts. Because all I wanted was to tell my ex-bestie to fuck off and never see her face on the property again. Except I couldn't do that at work.

A knock at the door saved me from saying anything I'd regret.

I turned to welcome the new guest and stilled.

Everything seemed to go into slow motion at the sight of Weston Wright filling up my doorframe.

"West?" I gasped.

He slung a hand up onto the top of the frame and

7

leaned forward through the door. He smirked, revealing the hidden dimple in his right cheek. "Hey, Nor."

The way he rolled over my name sent a thrill through my stomach. I hadn't seen my roommate in six months, when he'd left for LA with my brother to record his next album. The house was a temporary fix to the Tamara and August problem. I'd stay until he got back, and then I'd find another place.

Now, he was here.

Right here in front of me and looking somehow even more attractive than he had six months ago. He must have been working out because muscle bulked out from his towering frame. His already-broad shoulders were somehow bigger. The sharp lines of him were evident in the peak of muscle from his heather-gray T-shirt. It hung loose to his tapered waist. In contrast to the fitted black jeans that hugged his powerful thighs. But it all came back to that perfect face. The bright baby blues and razor-sharp jawline with a five o'clock shadow and that damn dimple.

I remembered the first time I'd met Weston. He'd driven into town to see his half-brothers, Jordan and Julian, who owned the winery with Hollin. I'd stumbled upon him with his hair all long and shaggy, blue eyes shining with uncertainty. He looked about as uncomfortable in dusty Wild West, West Texas as anyone I'd ever seen.

I'd been taken in, even then. Friends. We were friends. That was all we'd ever be. Because Weston Wright might be my roommate, but with the help of my brother, he was on the up-and-up in the music industry.

There was no way he was staying in Lubbock with all the opportunities open to him now. I would just keep reminding myself of that as I tried not to drool over him.

"West!" I cried as it sank in that he was really here.

I practically tripped over my feet to rush past Tamara and crash into Weston. His arms came around me as he laughed a deep rumble.

"You're home."

He released me with another smile. "Yep. Came straight here from the airport. Dropped Campbell off at Blaire's. He's been an uptight mess. He needs to get laid so bad."

I put my hands to my ears. "La, la, la. Do not need to know about my brother's sex life."

Weston ran a hand back through his hair, which was nearly back to the longish mess it had been that first day I saw him. He'd cut it super short when he first moved to Lubbock. He'd probably cut off the inch of curl at the ends any day now. "Sorry 'bout that."

"I know he's your best friend, but ew."

A throat cleared behind us. We both turned to find Tamara still standing there.

Her eyes took in Weston like a tasty snack. "Who's this, Nora?"

"Uh, this is my roommate."

Tamara arched an eyebrow. "Really?"

Weston stepped forward. "Sorry, didn't mean to interrupt a meeting." He stuck a hand out. "I'm Weston Wright."

"Wright," Tamara said with wide eyes. That name

9

held a lot of weight in our small town. The Wrights were Texas royalty. "I'm Tamara."

West jerked his hand back before Tamara could put hers into his. "Oh."

Tamara's mouth dropped open in shock at the insult. But Weston's eyes went straight to mine. He knew all about what had happened with August and Tamara. We'd lived together after it all went down. I'd been a wreck, crying myself to sleep most nights. He'd been there for me through all of it even though we hardly knew each other then.

"What are you doing here?" Weston snarled at Tamara.

And bless her heart, Tamara rushed into her spiel again. "I just got engaged! I was here to ask Nora to be the wedding planner for me and my fiancé, August."

"No," Weston snapped before she could get any further.

Tamara crossed her arms. Red rose up her neck and to her cheeks. "Excuse me?"

"Are you out of your goddamn mind? No fucking way is Nora going to plan a wedding for your snake ass."

"What?" she gasped. "How dare you!"

"No, how dare you! You put her through the wringer last year. You have no right to be here. What is *wrong* with you? Wasn't stealing her boyfriend enough for you? Do you have to continue to try to ruin her life?"

Tamara opened and closed her mouth like a fish.

"Get the fuck out," Weston said. He stepped back and pointed at the door.

"Well, I never..."

"Well, now, you have. Get the fuck out. *Now*."

And to my shock, Tamara went. She was flustered and angry, spouting obscenities at both of us, but she went.

As soon as she was gone, I burst into laughter. "Oh my God, I can't believe you did that!"

"I can't believe you didn't."

"I had it under control. I'd already told her that she couldn't have the wedding here, but I couldn't exactly tell her to fuck off at work. This was way more satisfying."

He laughed. "Yeah, I suppose so. Happy to oblige."

My hand landed on his wrist. "I'm glad you're home."

I suddenly realized we were mere inches from each other, alone in my office, and I hadn't seen him in months. Our eyes met in the small distance between us. I swallowed and pulled back.

"I mean..."

"I'm glad to be home, too," he agreed. "I missed you."

And though he meant as a friend and roommate, my heart tightened, and my stomach fluttered traitorously anyway. Because damn, I'd missed him too.

2

NORA

"You know, there are things called cell phones," I said with an arched eyebrow as I stuffed everything into my oversize work bag. "You could have called or texted to let us know you were coming home."

"I could have, but then I wouldn't have gotten to see your face when I showed up in your office." He slumped back in the chair across from my desk, kicking his feet up.

I brushed them off my desk. "LA has left you uncivilized."

He laughed. "That would be your brother."

I wrinkled my nose at him. "Campbell always was uncivilized, wasn't he? I never should have let you go off with him for six months. You're going to spend one night in the house and wreck all my progress."

"Progress?" he asked, jumping to his feet as I slung my bag on my shoulder, staggering slightly under the weight.

"I might or might not have been making some improvements."

"Improvements?" He looked stricken. "What did you do?"

"Guess you'll have to see when we get home, won't you?" I winked at him.

It had been silly to spend any time or energy on the house I was staying at, but it was impossible for me to live somewhere and not turn it into my own. It had been a nightmare to move out of the dorms because I had completely transformed my and Tamara's tiny suite into a girlie floral haven. I hadn't gone that far with West's place, but I'd had it to myself for six months. How could I resist a few dozen trips to HomeGoods?

"Is everything pink?"

"Maybe. What, are you not man enough for pink?"

"No, no, pink is definitely my color," he said with a grin in my direction.

"Good. It'd better be."

We headed out of my office and into the cellars of Wright Vineyard. It was a thriving operation. Last year, we'd won an award for Best in Class wine at an event in Austin. Hollin was taking our wine down to the show again this year in hopes of repeating the accomplishment. Plus, the weddings had *really* taken off after last year.

We'd had two huge weddings, including Morgan Wright—the CEO of Wright Construction, a Fortune 500 company—and her husband, Patrick's, event. That had been the highlight of the season. After that, wedding requests had skyrocketed. We had something at the vineyard nearly every Saturday. Hollin and I had even talked about bringing on another event planner since we were getting so much interest. At this point, I could handle it, but it was exciting to see that the vineyard had grown this much.

We'd made it to the cellars doors when they burst open, and my oldest brother, Hollin, strode toward us. "Nora, I just saw Tamara."

I kept my stride easy and light. "I know. I already spoke with her."

"I banned her from the premises. I don't know what the hell she was thinking."

"She and August got engaged."

Hollin gaped at me. "What the actual fuck?" He clenched his hands into fists. "I'll kill him."

"Not worth it," I assured him. "You got your punch in."

"You dated for three years, and he proposed to *her* in less than a year?"

I glared at my brother. "Yeah, I also was able to do the math."

"Not helping," Weston muttered.

That was when Hollin noticed him standing there. His jaw dropped. "West! Hey, I didn't know you were back in town."

"Yeah, I came in with Campbell today."

"That asshole didn't even tell me," Hollin growled.

"Me neither," I told him.

"Well, we finished our part on the album," Weston said. "There's some production stuff that still has to happen on the back end, but it's a wrap for us unless we need to go back for any rerecords."

"Fuck yes!" Hollin cried.

"Congratulations!" I said.

Weston grinned down at me. I knew how proud he was of all of this. Campbell was the lead singer of the band Cosmere that had skyrocketed into fandom a few years back. All that time spent bartending in LA had paid off, and now, he performed to sold-out stadiums all over the world. When his keyboardist had quit before their third album, he'd enlisted West's help. Weston wasn't an official part of the band, but he'd filled in on the whole album. He and Campbell had grown close, working together, and had been all but inseparable ever since.

"Yeah," he said, stuffing his hands into his pockets. "It's pretty cool."

"So, how long are you here?" Hollin asked the question I most wanted the answer to.

"Not sure. It's Campbell's birthday this weekend, and he wanted to spend it with Blaire. So, we took the first flight out of LA. We don't have anything to do for a while though. I don't think anyone is rushing to head back."

"Good. Y'all need the downtime," Hollin said.

"We should throw a surprise party," I rushed out.

Hollin snapped his fingers at me. "He'll hate that. Let's do it."

Weston snorted. "He will hate that. For someone in the spotlight, he sure hates it."

"Which will make it the best," I said with a laugh. "Something only siblings can get away with. I'll get together with Blaire to make sure he doesn't find out."

"Still bitter that you didn't get to plan their wedding, huh?" Hollin asked.

I scowled at him. "It wasn't cool."

"You were involved," Weston said.

"I know. I know. But eloping in Vegas is different than letting me create a huge, insane wedding and giving them exactly what they wanted. And before you say anything, I know that eloping was exactly what they wanted. But I can still be sad."

"Poor thing," Hollin said with a shake of his head. "I'll help with the surprise party. We can have it here."

"I'll help cover for you," Weston agreed.

"Done!" I did a little twirl in my high heels. "I love surprise parties."

"I don't know how you do that in those death traps," Hollin said.

I rolled my eyes at him. "Lots of practice." I hugged my brother. "We're going to head home early after dealing with Tamara."

"Sure thing. If you see Campbell, tell him he's an asshole," he said, shaking West's hand.

"Will do."

We headed out to the parking lot, where my CR-V sat next to Hollin's truck. I scanned the lot. "What did you drive?"

"Took an Uber from the airport. I left my car at the house."

"Right, right. Taking up that extra spot in the garage."

"What were you going to do with that extra spot?" He laughed and snagged the keys from my hand.

"Hey! I'm driving." I jumped for the keys, but he held them up over my head, so I couldn't get to them.

"No way, bite-sized," he joked.

I scoffed, my ears going hot at the nickname. He'd

used it when we first moved in together. I was about five feet flat and couldn't reach anything on the top shelves. He'd had to move everything I wanted to a lower shelf so that I could get to it. That was half the reason for the high heels all the time. Plus, they were *me* at this point.

"I'm fun-sized. Not bite-sized. Like a Snickers—soft on the outside, crunchy on the inside."

He snorted. "All right, Snickers. Let's go."

I rolled my eyes. Damn it! That wasn't a better nickname.

"Why must you drive?"

"I haven't had a car in six months, and LA traffic is shit. It's the little things."

I sighed. "Fine. I don't normally let anyone drive my SUV. You're lucky."

He dropped into the driver's side and then coughed. "Fuck." He shifted the seat all the way back to accommodate his long legs. He adjusted the mirrors and flicked the fuzzy pink dice in the rearview mirror. "Do you need luck because your feet can't touch the pedals?"

I rolled my eyes dramatically. "Course not. The luck is for everyone else on the road to survive my demon speeds."

Weston cracked up and shifted us into gear. "Yeah, I really missed you."

I flushed again as he peeled out of the parking lot. We listened to the local pop station on the way home, jamming out to Taylor Swift's latest. West spoke of the merits of her piano playing, and I sang the lyrics at the top of my lungs to drown out the shop talk.

He parked my SUV next to his Subaru, and I high-tailed it to the garage door.

"Okay, before you judge, remember that I didn't know you were coming home. I can change any of it."

He stood in front of me, brushing his hand against my side as he reached for the doorknob. "You're scaring me. What the hell did you do?"

I held my arms out to try to stop him from going inside. "Not yet. Let me explain."

But there was no way I could stop him from getting into his own house. He dropped his body down, throwing me over his shoulder like a sack of potatoes. His strong arm wrapped across the backs of my thighs. My bare thighs because I'd opted for a white skirt for work today. Oh God.

I screamed in shock as he lifted me and carried me over the threshold.

"West!"

"Stop wiggling, or I'll drop you."

"Put me down!"

He laughed as he stopped in the middle of the living room, freezing at the redecoration that I'd done to the space. "Snickers, what did you do?"

But he didn't sound upset as he gently set me back down onto my platforms. I brushed down my skirt, trying to cover the heat on my face and the heat...everywhere else, too.

"Well..." I whispered.

When Weston had left six months ago, the house had looked like a bachelor pad with an old couch, a coffee table dented from too many nights of quarters, a deformed beanbag, and an Xbox hooked up to a giant television. Since then, I'd reupholstered the entire couch with some light-gray fabric. It had taken three weekends to get the measurements right. I'd refinished the coffee table with wax and made the beanbag into a poof.

I'd begged a favor from an old Best Buy acquaintance to mount the television and hide all the cords in the wall. I'd purchased secondhand curtains for the bay window and refitted them to the space. Then, I'd filled the space with plants. Dozens of plants of every shape and size. Some hung from hooks in the ceiling. Others were in pots on little stands. Some were big enough to sit on the floor.

And...I'd painted the walls.

Every wall in the house that I had access to. I could only stare at beige for so long without going insane. And yes, the place was pink. Not as pink as my bedroom, but I had clearly designed the place for me and not for a dude.

"It's incredible. Is that my couch?" He looked gobsmacked.

"Yeah, I kind of fixed everything."

"And the plants. Holy shit, you have a green thumb."

"Sort of," I said, suddenly shy.

"Why did you think I'd hate this? It's awesome."

"Oh, well, uh, thanks. I just...you know, this was temporary, and I kind of took over. I don't have a place yet, but I can find something if you give me a weekend."

Weston blinked at me. "What are you talking about?"

"Well, I know you said that I could have the place while you were gone in LA and that it was, you know, a temp situation until I got back on my feet."

"Fuck, Nora, that's not what I meant! I thought you'd

want to leave. I left you an out in case you wanted to get your own place. I'm going to be back and forth from LA. So, I won't be here all the time anyway." He shrugged, a small smile hitting his features. "You can stay."

"You're sure?"

"I want you to stay." He grinned at me. "Stay."

"Okay," I said softly.

"That's a yes?"

I tipped my head down and bit my lip, trying to cover my excitement. "Yes. Yes, I'll stay."

3

WESTON

Telling her to stay was skating a dangerous line.

I knew that, even as I told her to stay. She was my best friend's little sister. She was my roommate. And she was also gorgeous.

Crossing that line was ill-advised.

To put it lightly, Campbell would probably murder me.

He and Hollin had warned me off Nora when we first agreed to move in together. They'd made themselves perfectly clear, and I'd given them my word that it wasn't like that with us. Which I was determined to stick by, even as she smiled up at me with her gorgeous heart-shaped face, Abbey blue eyes, and plump lips.

Best friend's little sister. I stamped the words on my brain as I stepped back.

"Good," I told her. "Did you touch my room?"

She laughed and shook her head. "No. I kept the door shut. I didn't touch the studio either."

"The drums are probably collecting dust."

"Well, I dusted last week. Didn't think it'd be good for the instruments."

I grinned. "Thanks, Nor." I took another step back from that smile. *Friends, roommates, best friend's little sister.* "I should go see Whitt and Harley."

"You haven't even seen your siblings?" She slipped out of her heels and was suddenly several inches shorter. She rocked back and forth on the balls of her feet. "Not that I'm going to see Campbell until he and Blaire are...finished."

"Wife," I offered as if that explained everything.

She waved me off and headed into the immaculately decorated living room. "Yeah. Yeah. Say hi to Whitt for me."

"You guys been hanging out?"

She shrugged. "Not really. You know how Whitt is."

I smirked. "Yeah. He's a bit uptight."

"I was unaware that twins could be complete and total opposites until I met you and Whitton."

"That's Whitt. Mr. Responsibility."

"I'm sure he kept y'all out of trouble."

"Don't be deceived. Whitt can get in just as much trouble. He just never gets caught."

She laughed. "I'll believe that when I see it."

"We'll get him drunk. That's when the best Whitt comes out," I assured her. "All right. I'll see you later."

She waved as I hurried back out of the house. Unlike Nora, who I'd wanted to surprise, I'd told Whitton and Harley that I was coming back into town. Whitt would not have been pleased with an ambush, and Harley was busy as a freshman at Texas Tech University. Her schedule was a nightmare. Between classes, her scholarship requirements, and her active party life, I'd be lucky to see her at all.

I slung on a jacket out, which I'd left behind since I didn't need it for perfect LA weather, and grabbed the keys to the Subaru. I'd gotten the Forester back in Seattle for a deal. She had nearly a hundred thousand miles on her and was still going strong. With all the money coming in from the Cosmere album, I might be able to replace her, but I hated the idea of it. We'd had a lot of good trips.

The drive to Wright Construction wasn't long, and then I was parking in the lot off campus. Whitton had gotten a job at the company that had our namesake by making a phone call. I still didn't know how I felt about it all, and Whitt felt weirder, but he wouldn't squander an opportunity when it looked him in the face.

Because two years ago, our entire lives had been flipped upside down. The three of us had grown up in Seattle with our mom, Tanya, and our dad, Owen. He'd given us his name, but they weren't married. As we'd gotten older, we had known that him living in Vancouver and showing up randomly to be with us was strange. A lot different than the other kids in our school. But we let it go.

Then, I decided to dig. What I found made me sick —*we* were dad's secret family.

He had two other sons, Jordan and Julian Wright, who had lived in Vancouver for most of their lives and recently moved to Lubbock, Texas, where the head of the corporation was. I emailed my half-brothers, and when I didn't get a response, I decided on a whim to drive over from a show I'd been playing in East Texas. Whitt had advised against it, but we got the truth that way.

After a year of back-and-forth about what to do, I decided to give this new life in Texas a shot. It ended up being the best thing I'd ever done. I'd met Campbell while working at a local studio and recorded a major album for the biggest band in the world.

One decision, and I had suddenly gotten everything I'd ever wanted.

I entered Wright Construction and took the elevator up to Whitt's office, knocking on his door. His head whipped up, and then he waved me in.

"About time," he said.

I shook my head at him. "Seriously? Not even a *welcome back*?"

Whitton shot me a twin look. "Welcome back."

"Now, you're just being a dick."

He arched an eyebrow. "Let me finish this email, and then we can go meet Harley."

I flopped back into the seat across from his desk, grabbing a pencil and flipping it between my fingers. Whitt gave me an insufferable look. But I saw the edges of his lips tug up.

We might be opposites. Whitt, the realist, to my dreamer. The suit to my rocker. The serious to my go with the flow. But he'd missed my wild energy as much as I'd missed his evenness. That was how it had always been.

"What do you think of the job?"

Whitt shrugged. "It's a job. I'm going to get a promotion next month."

"Yeah? You know already?"

"I'm doing three people's jobs. They'd be stupid not to move me up. Jordan said so anyway."

"How's it going, working for our brother?"

"*Half*-brother," Whitton snapped.

I held my hands up. "Fuck, Whitt, half-brother, if you must."

"I like him."

I snorted. "You don't sound like you do."

"He's a fair boss. Though I don't work directly under him."

"Nepotism and all."

"Look at you, remembering vocabulary," Whitton joked.

I flipped him off. "Anyway, Nora says hi."

Whitt's eyes flicked to mine. "Oh, yeah? You already saw her?"

"Surprised her at work."

"Uh-huh."

"Don't use that voice with me," I groaned.

"Don't do things that make me use that voice."

"I have done nothing."

Whitt went back to his email. "You like her?"

"Nah, come on, bro. She's my roommate."

"Right," he said, clicking a button.

"That's the voice again."

"Well, because I know you." Whitton hit another button and then nodded. "Email sent. Now, you can continue to annoy me on the way to see Harley."

"Finally." I jumped up and waited for Whitton to pull on his black suit coat before heading out of his office.

"So, Nora?" Whitton asked, heading toward his shiny silver Lexus instead of my baby Subi.

I regretfully followed him.

"She's cool, but she's also Campbell's little sister. He'd kill me if I looked at her wrong."

"That may be, but she seems to be a very genuine person. She's reached out a few times to help me acclimate to Lubbock."

Once we were in the car, he took off toward campus.

"She is. She decorated the entire house while I was gone. Which I shouldn't have even been surprised that you decided to get your own place, by the way."

"No, you shouldn't have. I like things a little more modern. A little more..."

I waved him off. "Yeah, yeah, we have different tastes."

"In women as well, which is how I know that Nora Abbey is right up your alley."

"No way," I lied. Because he was so fucking right, and it was dangerous to think about. "Have you met anyone?"

"I have not," he said. "A few dates, but nothing promising."

"No one crazy enough for you?"

Whitton, despite being the suit, had a thing for...well, I could only describe it as *batshit insane* girls. Like the more psychotic they were, the more he was into them. I wasn't sure if it was his actual type, but it was the only kind of girl I'd ever seen him pursue. And there wasn't a screening process for the level of crazy he was into.

"You're such a dick," Whitton said. "I don't look for crazy girls."

"Sure, Whitt."

He scowled at me as we pulled up to Thai Pepper. The line was already ten people deep in the hole-in-the-wall Thai place that had the best noodles I'd ever had in my life. We had excellent Thai in Seattle, and I'd been skeptical when Nora insisted we go here. But damn, she had been right.

Harley waved from a seat at the back of the restaurant. She was in a black miniskirt with ripped fishnets and Doc Martens, paired with a white leather jacket that might have been one of my old ones. Her long, freshly dyed, blonde hair was in two pigtails, her eyes were heavily lined, and she had on bubblegum-pink lipstick. Oh, Harley.

We pushed through the space to where she was.

"West!" she cried, throwing her arms around me.

She was nearly six feet tall but didn't hide behind her height. She never slumped or refused to wear heels or anything. She took up as much space as she wanted, and I loved that about her.

"Hey, Harley."

"I'm glad you're back. How was LA?"

Whitt hugged her next, and then we took the seats opposite her.

"Oh, and I already ordered for the table."

"Thanks," Whitton said.

"LA was great. Just wrapped the album. Best work of my life."

"I bet it is," she said enthusiastically. "I cannot wait to hear it. When do I get an early copy? Also, can I meet Yorke? Because hello!"

"No!" Whitt said automatically.

"That sounds like a bad idea," I agreed.

Yorke was another member of Cosmere. He played guitar, was usually silent unless it mattered, and had an avid following called the Peppermint Patties.

She sighed and slumped back. "Y'all are no fun."

Whitton froze. "Are you using Southern phrases now?"

"Well, I'm Southern!" Harley said, leaning in just to irritate him.

"You've lived in Texas for six months."

"Yeah, but Dad is from here, which means we're from here, which means I get to say it. I find that way better than *you guys* or something fucking gendered. At least *y'all* is neutral. You can say it about any group of people. We don't have to be so goddamn binary."

Whitton looked at me in panic. "This is what you've missed."

"Our little sister, all grown up."

"I wouldn't go that far," Whitt grumbled.

"Anyway, when are you going back?" Harley asked. "Can I come with?"

"I don't know when I'm going back. I have a standing offer on the table as a producer for the studio. They loved my work with Cosmere and said they could take me on full-time."

"That sounds like a solid job," Whitton said.

"Yeah. It would be, but I don't know. I feel like there's so much happening right now, and I'm not ready to be tied down to just one thing."

"What's the five-year plan? What do you want out of all of this?" Whitt asked.

I knew the answer to that, but it was essentially impossible. I wanted to join Cosmere. But their keyboardist, Michael, had *just* quit, and he'd been with the band for years. I couldn't imagine them ever replacing him. Not with how it had all gone down. I was a fill-in, but I wasn't the real deal. That didn't stop me from dreaming.

"I can't think about a five-year plan, Whitt. Jesus, did you think we'd be *here* five years ago?"

Just then, our food showed up. Whitton had curry while Harley and I had pad thai. Though hers was as hot as they could possibly make it. She was obsessed with spicy food.

"I certainly didn't think I'd be at Tech," Harley said. She twirled her food around on her chopsticks.

"Regardless," Whitton said, "just because we didn't see Lubbock happening to any of us doesn't mean we can't plan for the future."

"Dude, that's you. Not me," I told Whitt. "I want to go with the flow."

Whitton's eyes twitched at that word.

"In five years, I want to be in law school," Harley announced. "There, Whitt, you can stop hassling West on the first day home."

"I'm not hassling. I'm being practical," Whitt argued.

"Well, stop being practical then," Harley said with a laugh. "Or I'll put one of these ghost peppers in your curry."

Whitton shot her a look. "Harlyn Anne, you wouldn't dare."

"We're throwing a surprise party," I interjected before

they could get started. They could go like this for hours if I let them.

"Party!" Harley said. "Can I come?"

"No," Whitton said at the same time I said, "Yes."

"She's nineteen," Whitton argued.

"It's Campbell's birthday. Everyone is invited, and she doesn't have to drink."

"Y'all don't have to be so ridiculous. I'm in college. I'm at frat parties every weekend. I've had alcohol before."

"I'll be there," Whitton said.

"Me too," Harley agreed.

I laughed at them both and went back to my food. It was good to be home with my siblings. I was used to being out on the road with other bands and away from them for months on end, but it was great, coming back to them. And I couldn't wait to be with all my friends at the party.

4

NORA

Planning a surprise party for Campbell with three days' notice was a feat. Luckily, we didn't have a wedding that weekend at Wright Vineyard, and I had a few days of planning time to get it up and running.

"So, you'll get the cake?" I asked Blaire.

My sister-in-law—which was still crazy to think about —smiled and nodded. Her bangs were long enough to flutter into her eyes with the movement. "I have it covered."

"And he doesn't suspect a thing?"

"Nope. I told him I have something special planned for his birthday. I think he's hoping for sex."

Her best friend and Hollin's girlfriend, Piper, snorted. "Isn't he always?"

"Aren't all guys like that?" Blaire shot back.

Piper grinned devilishly, her eyes shifting to Hollin's. "I suppose so."

"Gross, y'all. Those are my brothers!"

Both girls snickered.

We were all standing in my dad, Gregg's, backyard. Dad wanted to have a big *welcome home* and *congratulations* thing for Campbell. He and Campbell hadn't always exactly gotten along. They'd had a lot of grief after Mom died, because Campbell had been Mom's favorite, and he'd blamed Dad for her running out. But it had been a horrific car accident that had taken her life. It had been no one's fault. Years of therapy had gotten us all to that point. So Campbell and Dad were trying, and that was what mattered.

Our aunts, Lori and Vail, stood together by the barbecue as Vail whipped up her famous burgers. Jordan and Julian's mom, Helene, sat in a chair next to them. She'd had cancer a few years back, and she still seemed fragile all the time. But the doctors had said she was stable. It was nice to have everyone together.

"Weston said he'd help if you needed a way to get Campbell to the winery," I offered.

"That would be great." Blaire set her hand on my arm. "How is living with him, by the way? I know you said that you liked having the house to yourself."

"I did. I thought he wanted me to leave, but he said that I could stay. Misunderstanding. And I know it's only been a few days, but it's kind of nice to have a roommate."

"A cute roommate," Piper added.

I flushed. "Well, yeah. Those Wrights, you know?"

"We know," Blaire and Piper said together and then giggled.

"So, are you two..." Piper trailed off with emphasis and a wink.

"Uh, no, just roommates."

"Come on," she groaned. "After what August did…"

Piper had been there the day that I'd caught August cheating on me. She'd helped Hollin take care of me and had been hinting for the last several months that I should get back out there. That was all well and good, but how did one begin to get *out there*? I had never dated before. I had no clue where to begin. I wasn't lucky enough to stumble upon another guy again, like I had with August. And anyway, look at how that had ended.

"Piper," Blaire chastened.

"Sorry. I didn't mean to bring him up. I just want you to be happy."

"Thanks. It's fine. Anyway, party planning makes me happy. So, let me know if you need anything else for Monday."

"What's happening Monday?" Campbell asked, suddenly appearing at Blaire's side and sliding an arm around her waist.

She giggled and turned into him. He pressed a kiss firmly to her lips. A good distraction. And I was happy for them, happy to see both of my brothers happy. I wanted that for them. I wanted it for me, too.

"Don't change the subject," he said against her lips.

"You kissed me," she teased.

"Get a room," Piper grumbled.

Campbell winked at her.

He asked his wife another question, but my phone dinged in my pocket. I pulled it out, planning to silence it. Then, I saw the name on the screen, and my stomach dropped out of my body.

August.

I swallowed and swiped on the message.

Hey, can we meet? Tamara told me that she came to see you, and I just need to apologize.

I shouldn't respond. He'd been messaging me on and off since we broke up. At first, I'd answer his messages, and we'd text for days before I got mad all over again. I was sure Tamara had no idea that he'd done that. But eventually, I'd refused to answer. It hadn't made it any easier because the messages still came.

We shouldn't meet.

Nora, please...

No. It's a bad idea. I don't need an apology.

Which was a lie. I wanted one desperately. I wanted it to all go back to how it had been. Even though it was impossible.

No, but you deserve one. What happened...fuck, Nora, please let me do this in person. It won't be right through text. You know it won't. And you deserve better from me.

I closed my eyes against those words. Ones I'd wanted so bad earlier. And yet they were always going to be false.
But...I wanted to see him.
I didn't want to be that girl.
But ugh!

I'm at my dad's with my brothers. You can't come here.

Meet me at the park.

I glanced around at the party. Blaire had successfully distracted Campbell. Hollin had wandered over to put his arm around Piper. Dad was arguing with Vail about the burger situation. Everyone was distracted. I could probably slip away for a minute.

I squeezed my eyes shut. Was it so wrong to want to see him? I wouldn't have to do it again. Not ever. Fuck.

Fine. You have five min utes.

I made some excuse about taking a phone call and slipped back through my dad's house. I snagged my jacket as I exited through the front door and strode toward the park across the street.

August hadn't had to say *where* in the park to meet. When we'd been together, we always used to meet at the swings on family holidays. I sank into the swing and pushed off, letting it rock back and forth on its own. I felt stupid. I was *being* stupid.

It didn't change how I felt to acknowledge that this was the last thing I should be doing. I was still sitting here on a swing, waiting for my ex-boyfriend, who was now engaged to someone else. I knew how dumb that was. But I would just let him say whatever he was going to say, and then I'd tell him not to contact me anymore. I might even get brave enough to block his number.

A throat cleared behind me. I dragged my feet in the

dirt and turned around.

August strode toward me in his black peacoat, his hair perfectly put together, a tentative smile on his lips. "Hey, Nora."

I swallowed back all the pain at seeing him, knowing he wasn't mine. "Hi."

"Thanks for meeting me."

I crossed my arms over my chest. "This is the last time."

He nodded. "I figured."

"It's not fair to ask this of me, you know?"

"I know. I fucked up, but I didn't want you to suffer."

I scoffed. "You should have thought of that before you cheated on me."

He kicked a rock in front of him, looking down at his feet. "Yeah. I know I can't make up for that."

"Make up for it? You're marrying the girl you cheated on me with."

He winced. "Uh, yeah. She really wanted to get married."

I took a step back in disgust. Was he blaming *Tamara* for the engagement? How typical. "You still proposed."

"Yeah. I'm sorry she came to see you." He took a step forward, closer. "I, uh, I never knew she would do something like that. Of course we're not going to get married at the vineyard or have you plan it."

"No, because I told her *no*."

"She said that you had"—he cleared his throat—"another guy with you, who cussed her out." His eyes met mine again.

"Are you here to find out if I'm *seeing* someone?" I

asked in disbelief.

"No, no. I'm here to apologize."

"Jesus, August," I said, storming away from him and running a hand back through my hair.

Here he was, literally engaged to my ex-bestie, and he was trying to figure out if I was dating someone. What a pathetic, egotistical, narcissistic ass.

"I can't do this. I should have never come here."

"Nora, wait," he called as I stormed back toward my dad's house.

"I waited for you. I'm done waiting. I'm done with all of this."

He grasped the sleeve of my jacket and dragged me to a stop. "I'm so sorry. For everything. For Tamara and the engagement and hurting you. Fuck."

"That's not *good enough*," I snarled at him. I jerked my arm away from him. "Your words mean absolutely nothing when they aren't backed up by any actions." I shoved him away from me. "Stop apologizing. Stop this puppy-dog act. Go home to your *fiancée*, August, because if you contact me again, I'm going to tell her about all of it."

His face paled. We both knew exactly what Tamara would do if she found out he'd come to see me, let alone that he'd still been texting me all these months.

"Nora, hey, don't do this."

"I'm done." A tear slid down my cheek, and I angrily swiped it away. I hated that it had happened in front of him. I'd sworn no more tears. "I'm done."

Then I walked away, and he let me go. As he'd done many times before.

5

NORA

"Don't go," Campbell said. "I only just got home."

"I know. Work is work though," I said, wincing slightly at the lie. "This couple is pretty demanding."

As much as I wanted to hang out at Campbell's return party, I couldn't stay here another minute. Not after August. And telling my brothers about it would end in bloodshed.

"You sure you're okay, shrimp?"

I nodded and hoped it was convincing. "Totally." I hefted my phone. "Just work. You know?"

He ruffled my hair lightly. "Well, come out for my birthday at least. Blaire said she got a reservation. Ask her for the details."

"I will."

At least that made me smile. I'd worried that he'd caught on to what we were doing, but so far, so good. I'd be composed again by then. I needed time alone to deal with what had happened.

I waved at the girls and Hollin and then fled the scene. I was halfway home when I remembered that I wasn't going home to an empty house.

"Fuck," I whispered.

I'd planned to snag some ice cream and unleash my tears, but I didn't exactly want West to hear that. It was one thing to cry alone, but another thing entirely for someone to see me still mourning this bullshit. August had demolished my life, and I still didn't know how to get over it.

My heart ached at the thought. Why couldn't I move on like anyone else? Ten months was long enough to suffer, wasn't it?

With a sigh, I abruptly turned the wheel down the next street and veered into the parking lot of my favorite nursery—Apple's Nursery. Apple was the owner's nickname for his wife, who had been working by his side at the place for thirty years. She was adorable and always so helpful. We'd gotten real fond of each other. Despite that fact, I avoided the front, not ready to face anyone I knew, and meandered down the aisles of greenery.

I hadn't gotten into plants until after Weston left. I'd wanted to get a kitten or a puppy, but my wedding days were *long*. It felt cruel to leave a pet home alone all day. But plants? *Plants* I could keep alive. And it had gone from one potted monstera, which I'd been assured was nearly impossible to kill, to a veritable trove of greenery.

At the back of the place, I found a single orange flowering plant—a clivia, if my research was correct. It bloomed at the end of February and into March with the prettiest sunset flowers. I needed a sunset today.

I took the clivia up to the front and found Apple waiting for me.

"Plant therapy?" she asked intuitively.

"Nothing fixes your problems quite like buying another plant."

Apple laughed softly. "A girl as pretty and young as you can't have too many problems."

My lips wobbled. "I wish that were true."

"Still having boy trouble?"

"Yeah," I admitted. "Just trying to move on, but my ex is now engaged to that girl."

"The one he left you for?" Apple asked with a gasp.

I nodded. "Yeah."

"How foolish of him." Apple put her hand on mine. "Chin up, dear. You're much better than that young man. You don't need him. You need to find someone else who sees how brightly you shine."

"Thanks, Apple."

"And come back by to see me soon."

I promised that I would and then headed back to my car. The new plant did make me feel better, but Apple's words echoed in my head. I wanted to forget August, but how the hell did I even begin to find someone new?

That was a mystery I had no clue how to solve, but at least I was calmer by the time I got back to Weston's house. When I stepped inside, my cheeks heated, and I nearly dropped my plant. Well, damn. Weston Wright had been working out because he was currently in nothing but basketball shorts, and he was *ripped*. I swallowed as my eyes traveled down the six-pack and to the V that disappeared into his shorts.

"Nora!" he said, popping the top on a Coke. "You're home early."

"Yeah." I blinked and forced myself to look at anything else. It was hard to pull my gaze elsewhere, but then I took in the rest of the kitchen and realized he was cooking. "You're making dinner?"

"Uh, yeah, lasagna. Did you eat at your dad's?"

"I didn't actually." I set the clivia down on the table and shrugged out of my jacket. "I left before burgers."

"Really? Why?"

I looked at my feet. "I don't want to talk about it."

"All right," he agreed easily. "You want some lasagna? It's almost done."

"That would be...nice. It smells amazing." My mouth watered as he pulled it out of the oven.

"Thanks. It's my mom's recipe. She's Italian, and she was firm on making sure we all knew how to cook the basics, you know?"

My stomach dropped at the words. "I kind of missed that with my mom."

His gaze snapped to mine. "Sorry..."

I waved him off. I'd been a freshman in high school when Mom died. I'd had a long time to come to terms with her car accident, but it still sometimes hit me in the chest how much I'd lost and missed out on. Especially when I was already down. "You don't have to apologize. I can't get her back, and it's been a long time. I want to hear about your mom."

"Well," he said, dishing us each a plate, "I miss her, but we talk on the phone every week."

"You do?"

He nodded. "She got a new job, working at a corporate office in Seattle. We asked her to come to Lubbock, but she's always lived in Seattle. I'm not sure she'd do it unless one of us had a kid."

I sputtered, "That would be something."

"For real. Plot twist."

I took a seat opposite him and dug into the lasagna. "Holy shit!" I groaned with a full mouth.

"You like it?"

"Like?" I asked after I swallowed. "Try *love*. This is unbelievable."

"Thanks. You should try my mom's. It's way better."

"No way. This is...a godsend."

"I'm glad you like it." He gestured to our new plant. "What's this about?"

"I'm turning into a plant lady."

He snorted. "That ship has sailed."

"True," I admitted as I shoveled pasta into my mouth. But Weston was still looking at me with a thoughtful expression on his face. As if he already knew that something had happened. "What?"

"Nothing," he said automatically. "Just...Campbell texted and said to check on you, that you seemed off."

"He did not!"

Weston chuckled. "Oh no, your brother cares about you," he said sarcastically.

"I know he cares, but...ugh! How did he even know?"

"I don't know. He said that you lied about work, but he just let you go."

I groaned. "Great."

"Could be worse."

I waved my fork at him. "I doubt Whitt interferes in *your* life."

Weston nearly choked on his bite. "Are you kidding me? All Whitt does is meddle. He literally asked me about my five-year plan the minute I saw him."

I couldn't help it; I laughed. "Seriously? You just got back."

"Trust me, Harley and I dug into him."

"How is your sister doing?"

"Four-point-oh last semester. Honor roll. Research assistant," Weston said with pride. "She's coming to Campbell's party tomorrow."

"It'll be good to see her. She's a badass."

He shook his head. "She's something." Then, his eyes met mine again. "That was a clever turn of subject. You going to tell me what's actually going on?"

I blew out a harsh breath. "Not going to let it go?"

"Nope."

"I saw August today."

West stilled. "Why?"

"He wanted to apologize for what Tamara did at the winery."

"I hope you told him to fuck off," he practically growled.

"Basically," I admitted. I threw my fork into the bowl and sat back. "I was so mad at myself for even seeing him. It's utter bullshit that he can even draw me back in like that. I don't want to feel like this anymore, but I don't know what to do. Everyone says to move on, as if it were that easy."

"It's not easy after everything you went through with

him, but I have to agree. He's not worth holding on to like this."

"I know he isn't." I blinked back tears and glanced away. "Look, I want to move on. I want to date someone else. I want all of that, but how do I do it?" I swallowed and finally admitted what I'd been holding in. "I've only ever dated one person before. I don't know what I'm doing."

He stared at me in shock for a second. "You've only been with August?"

I briskly nodded once. "Yep. For three years. In high school, everyone was too afraid of my brothers. In college, it was always Tamara who got the dates. And now I'm so *awkward* around guys."

He laughed softly. "Come on. It can't be that bad."

"Oh yeah? I downloaded Tinder while you were gone and went on exactly one date, where the guy *bailed* before dinner was even finished."

"What a douche."

"How do people know what to do? Give me an event to plan, and I can take charge so easily, but dating?" I huffed. "I don't know the first thing about dating. I wish there were like...a flirt coach." I reached for my drink. The idea began to grow in my mind. A flirt coach was exactly what I needed. "I need someone who can teach me how to flirt and date and all that. Someone who can make me not be so incredibly awkward and shy around guys."

Weston leaned back in his seat and looked at me thoughtfully for a few seconds.

"What?" I asked self-consciously. "Is it a dumb idea?"

"I'll do it."

I blinked. "Do what?"

"I can show you how to flirt and date."

He was serious. I could see that on his face, and yet I couldn't believe it. The Weston, who had left six months ago, had been a little quiet and shy. The only things he'd cared about were family and music. I'd noticed that he'd come back more confident. I'd assumed that LA had rubbed off on him. I hadn't considered that had probably come with six months of girls, too.

My cheeks heated slightly. "Qualifications?"

He shrugged. "I was trained by the best." I arched an eyebrow. "Your brother."

"You're going to teach me how to flirt by using what my brother taught *you*? That seems like he'd hate it."

"When I was in LA, things got a little...wild. I've never been a big drinker because alcoholism runs in my family, but I let loose in LA. Campbell laughed his ass off at my attempts to flirt. Having the biggest rockstar in the world as your wingman gives you a confidence boost. And so I... flirted...a lot."

He shrugged and arched an eyebrow at me, as if I'd have anything to say about it. We weren't anything but roommates. He had no reason to hide the fact that he'd probably hooked up with dozens of girls in LA. But still, I blushed at the thought.

"So, now you're a pro?"

"Something like that. You need to put yourself out there and have someone help you through it. I can be that person."

"And you won't tell Campbell?"

"I don't want him to punch me in the face. So, no."

I bit my lip. What was the harm here? Weston would teach me. I'd put myself out there to possibly get hurt all over again. But it would be worth it to get over August. That was the only goal here.

So, I nodded. "All right. When do we start?"

Weston pushed his chair back. "Tonight."

"What?" I squeaked.

"Look, it's now or never. The more time you have to think about it, the more likely you'll back out. So, let's just go out tonight."

I gulped. "Uh, okay. This is going to be...fun."

He laughed. "Don't worry, Snickers. By the time I'm done with you, every single guy in Lubbock will be after you."

I nodded but couldn't help wondering if that meant *him*, too.

PART II

FLIRT COACH

6

NORA

Weston was right about one thing—I was already second-guessing myself.

I'd changed into a black dress and my favorite pair of red-bottomed heels, which I only pulled out when I needed moral support. Now, we were in Weston's Subaru, driving downtown, and I had no idea if this was the right thing to do.

Me, pick up guys? Learn how to flirt? Let loose?

It seemed...impossible.

And yet here I was, fidgeting up a storm, but still on my way to do it.

"Are you sure about this?"

He'd thrown on dark jeans, a black T-shirt, and a bomber jacket before we left. His hair fell forward into his eyes when he looked at me. "Are *you* sure? We don't have to do this, but I'm here for you if you want."

"I..." I didn't know what I wanted. I wanted to be over August. I was so pissed at him for everything he'd done, and I didn't know how to do it alone. "Are you sure I'll be able to learn?"

"Yeah, I'm sure. You just need the nudge to do it."

"Okay. Yeah." I swallowed down my fear and tilted my chin up. "Yes. I want to do it."

He must have seen the resolve on my face because he nodded. "All right. What's your experience in a bar situation? I'm sure you've had a guy buy you a drink. Get your number?" He glanced over at me, and I was already shaking my head. "Really? I find that hard to believe."

"I've never even had a guy buy me a drink. I mean, besides August," I added lamely.

"How? How is that possible?"

"Tamara," I whispered the word. "She was always the center of every situation. Sometimes, she got drinks for both of us, but it was never me."

"Hmm," he said, rubbing a hand along the scruff across his jaw. "Well then, that's our goal tonight. A guy to buy you a drink and ask for your number."

"And how do I do that?"

"Honestly, for women, it's so much easier. All you have to do is put yourself out there. If you're hot and smile at a guy, it's pretty likely he'll come over and talk to you to buy you a drink."

I blinked at him. "It is *not* that easy."

He laughed as he pulled into the parking lot of Flips. "It really is."

I hopped out of the car and walked around to meet him on the other side. "So, I just stand here?"

The night was dark, and stars sparkled overhead, dulled by the soft light pollution in the city. It was only bright enough to illuminate the sharp contours of his jaw as he stepped in close to me.

"Like this." His arm brushed against mine. I shivered at the contact as our eyes met. "Hey. I'm Weston. Haven't seen you here before."

I blinked up at him at his nearness. Our bodies were so close together. "Hi," I breathed.

He towered over me, and I had to tilt my head up to get a good look at his face. My heart was pounding in my chest. And suddenly, the entire world disappeared. It was just the two of us, standing in a packed parking lot.

"I'm...I'm Nora," I offered.

"Nora," he said with a certain look and a smile. "I like that."

"Thanks." I tucked a lock of my hair behind my ear and broke eye contact as my face flushed. Somehow, even here, in this pretend situation, I could get embarrassed.

Weston reached out and tilted my head back up to look at him. "Don't hide from me."

I gulped. "I...wasn't."

"Pretend this is an event you planned," he encouraged. "You're in charge. This is your world now."

My spine straightened at those words. This was just another event I'd put together. This was my domain. I existed here. A confident smile came to my face. "I'm ready."

Weston's eyes dipped to my lips, and then he dropped his hand, stepping back and nodding. He cleared his throat. "Better." He stuffed his hands into his pockets. "Let's get you inside and try it out. Hold on to that energy."

I took a step away from him, afraid that I'd pushed him away. We'd been so close and then so, so far away. My stomach twisted in confusion. Weston was helping me. That was all this was, but still, when he'd lifted my chin, everything had gone blissfully silent.

Flips was the best option for this little experiment because it wasn't the kind of bar I'd frequented when I was a Texas Tech undergrad. Tamara and I were all about Cricket's and Chimy's. We'd prowl Broadway, laughing, drunk on cheap booze. All those memories were now tainted with a sheen of blue. The ache of her betrayal and pain of knowing I could never get any of those years back.

Flips was known for their lunchtime hot-dog menu. At night, it transformed into the perfect dive bar, complete with a long bar on the far side of the room and pool tables at the back. The place was packed, and no one paid any mind to Weston and me stepping inside.

"See if you can grab a seat. I'll get us drinks. What do you like?"

"Uh...whatever you want."

Weston shook his head. "Always have a drink request. Someone is going to ask you what you want, and you should know automatically. I could give you something you don't like or something full of alcohol, where one drink would knock you on your ass. You don't want anything from that kind of guy."

I blinked. "Right. I'll take a Revolver."

Weston's eyebrows rose. "A beer?"

"Yeah? I like their Blood & Honey." I arched an eyebrow. "Is that a problem?"

"No, just pictured you as a fruity-drink kind of girl."

"I have two older brothers," I said with a shrug. "Learned from the best."

He considered that for a second before nodding. "Blood & Honey it is."

Weston disappeared in the crowd near the bar while I looked for a table. Literally every surface in the entire place was full. It was so crammed that I could barely find wall space, let alone a table. After a few minutes, I gave up on finding an open spot and shifted into a corner, where I could watch the bar.

A minute later, Weston appeared with two beers. He passed one to me.

"Thanks," I said, taking a good long sip to calm my nerves.

"Sure. No tables?"

"Nothing. We picked the right night, I guess. It's slammed. I could barely walk around in here. How'd you get the beer so fast?"

"I know the bartender. Pete came into the studio some when I worked there."

"Look at you, acting like a local."

West grinned. "Sure. *Me*, a Lubbock local."

"You skipped the line at the bar," I reminded him.

He laughed. "I suppose I did. Now, it's your turn."

I drained my Blood & Honey. West arched an eyebrow at me.

I tipped the empty bottle at him. "Liquid courage."

Then, I passed it back to him and headed to the bar. I felt ridiculous. But I thought about everything West had told me. I needed to work the bar like I would if I were at one of my events. I was hardly shy on a good day, but somehow, when it came to boys, I completely froze up. Just like I had under Weston's gaze.

I squeezed my way to the front of the busy bar. I stared up at the chalk menu as if I were contemplating what to order. Then, I shifted to observe the people all around me. It was mostly guys, but none of them were looking at me. And I didn't know how to get their attention. Suddenly, my throat closed, and I felt so very small. How had I thought I could do this? I wasn't ready for this big of a step. I should go home and give up on finding a guy who was into me. Or get on Tinder and suffer through bad dates. I shuddered at that thought.

"What'll you have?"

I jerked my eyes up as Pete, the bartender, looked directly at me. I'd been stuck in my own head and not even realized that it was my turn.

"I'm still deciding," I told him.

He nodded at me. "Sure thing." He pointed at the guy next to me. "You?"

"I'll take a Miller Lite." The guy glanced over at me as Pete went to grab his beer. "Hey, have we met before?"

I met his gaze and frowned, considering it. He did sort of look familiar. "Um, I'm not sure."

"I'm sure I've seen you around."

I tapped my lip, trying to place his face, but I saw so many faces at my job that they sometimes all blurred together. "I work at Wright Vineyard. Do you ever go by there?"

"That must be it," he agreed. "I love that place." He stuck his hand out. "I'm Cannon."

"Nora," I said, shaking his hand.

Pete plunked his drink down. "That all?"

Cannon pointed at me. "Whatever she's having."

"Oh," I said in wonder. I'd thought that he was just being nice. Had he been...flirting with me? Had he ever actually seen me before? Was that a line? Wow, I was bad at this. "I'll take a Blood & Honey."

"Good taste," Cannon said.

Pete brought the beer to me, and Cannon dropped cash on the bar.

"Um, thanks for this," I said.

"No problem. Me and my buddies are playing pool. If you want to play a game, come join us."

He winked at me and then disappeared.

A small thrill ran through me as I headed back to where Weston was waiting. I did a little jig as I walked back to him.

"Oh my God, I *did* it!" I twirled in place, nearly falling over in my heels.

Weston laughed and reached for me. "Someone bought you a drink?"

"Yes! He's playing pool over there. Should I go talk to him again?"

Weston glanced at the guys I pointed out and wrinkled his nose. "Yeah, probably not. This is just practice. Let's not get attached to the frat boys."

I snorted. "Not my type anyway. But he was nice! And he bought me a drink."

"See, I told you it was easy once you got started."

"I didn't really do anything though. He did everything. I didn't even realize he was flirting with me."

West laughed. "Yeah. That was the story of my life,

too, but you'll be able to pick it out the more practice you have. See if you can get a guy to ask for your number."

"How do I do that?"

"Just talk about your life."

My eyes widened. "Uh, you make it seem like that's simple."

"It is."

"You're a musician. So, of course it is."

He tipped his drink at me. "Fair."

"So, just...regale them with descriptions of my plants and being a wedding planner?"

He nearly choked on his drink. "Maybe hold off on talk of being a plant lady and wedding bells until the first date." I rolled my eyes at him. "What did you say to that guy?"

"I don't know. I mentioned Wright Vineyard."

"There. That's your opening. Try that again."

I bit my lip and glanced at the bar again as I sipped my beer. That had been surprisingly easier than I'd thought. And a little confidence boost. All I'd had to do was fake being confident, and I hadn't even done that well. Maybe I *could* do this.

I finished off my second beer. "Should I try again?"

Weston brushed a strand of hair off my face. "Knock 'em dead."

7

WESTON

There was only one problem with this situation.

It was working.

Nora was shy around guys. That fact was still clear. But it didn't seem to matter. Once I'd forced her to wade out into the deep end, she'd figured out how to swim. Every adorable stagger brought her right back to me with another beer in hand, giggling about the stupid thing that the guy had said or how she'd managed to get through the conversation. She still hadn't had anyone ask for her number, but she was on her fourth beer, and I'd only purchased the first.

"I did it," she crooned as she stumbled into me. Literally.

I caught her around the middle, swung her around, and pressed her back against the wall. She gave a little hiccup, and then covered her mouth.

"I did it."

"Did what?" I asked, suddenly conscious that I had her pressed against a wall.

My body leaned into her with an arm wrapped protectively around her waist. She was all soft and supple under me. And despite sending her off after other guys all night, I'd had a good night. Her coming back to me and recounting it all. Always back to me, doing her ridiculous little dance.

She held up her beer. It wasn't Blood & Honey, which meant it was beer five. "Gave out my number."

"Really? Who?"

She pushed my shoulder lightly and pointed out the guy. He was another frat bro, like the first, with a backward baseball cap and a popped collar. It was just practice, but I didn't like the idea of that guy hitting on her.

"His name is Chip."

"Of course it is."

She giggled again. "Do I go out with him?"

"Nah. Just practice, Snickers."

She tipped her head back. "This has actually been fun, West. Thanks for taking me out here."

"You're welcome. I'm glad I could help."

Her bright blue eyes looked up at me. She wasn't even trying to flirt with me. She had no idea what those eyes were doing to me, looking up at me under thick, dark lashes. A half-smile on her painted lips.

I swallowed and tried to focus on anything other than my cock twitching in my pants. I did not need to feel this right now. She'd had her heart broken, and the last thing she needed was for me to make any of this harder. Not to mention, Campbell and Hollin had made it clear that nothing was going to happen there. I wasn't sure they'd ever forgive me if I touched her. I was pretty sure they'd kill me if I hurt her. I couldn't take that chance.

So, I backed up.

Way up.

Put all the distance I needed between me and her. Told my cock to fucking sort its shit out. Nora Abbey wasn't for me. She couldn't be.

"We should get you home."

"What?" she gasped. "It's early. I should practice more."

"You're a little drunk."

"Shouldn't that make it easier?"

"Maybe. But we want to keep you safe. We can practice more later."

She shrugged. "You're the boss." Then, she passed me her half-finished drink. "If I finish that, I'll be wasted anyway."

"Five is your limit?"

She winked at me. "That's seven."

I arched an eyebrow. "How did I miss two?"

"I drank them at the bar," she said, pushing off the wall and teetering slightly.

Well, that explained a lot. I'd thought that she seemed a little drunk, but I didn't know where her tolerance was. Mine had always been strong despite not drinking much before going to LA. Another thing I'd gotten from my dad. Great.

"Come on, you," I told her. I wrapped an arm around her and steered her toward the door.

We were almost out when a guy reached for her. "Nora! You're leaving already?"

It was the guy, Chip, who she'd given her number to.

"Yeah, Chip. Time for me to call it a night."

Chip eyed me for a second and then dismissed me. "I can give you a ride home later if you want. I thought we were having a good time."

"She said no," I growled low, putting Nora between me and *Chip*.

I didn't know what had come over me, but I didn't want him anywhere *near* her. It was almost...possessive-ness...or jealousy.

The guy held his hands up. "Hey, tough guy, I was talking to the lady."

"West, it's fine," Nora said, putting her hand on my arm. "Let's just go home."

"This your boyfriend?" Chip asked in confusion.

Nora laughed. "No, no, no. Just a friend."

I arched an eyebrow at him, and Chip backed off.

"Cool. Friend. Right," he said. "I'll call you."

Nora waved at him and then strode out of the bar. "That was *weird*," she said. "Why was he acting like that?"

Him and not me. Well, at least that was a relief.

"Pretty sure he bought you drinks, hoping to get you home," I told her.

"Oh," she said with a nod. "Right. I'm not really inter-ested in that."

I breathed out slowly. Although I was teaching her how to flirt and getting her out there to date, I wasn't sure how much I could handle like having her bring guys home on the regular.

The thought sent a chill through me. Yeah, I didn't like that idea *at all*.

I helped Nora into the passenger seat and then drove us back home. If possible, she was even drunker by the time we got there. As if that last drink had hit her *hard* on the drive. She kicked her shoes off and carried them inside as she stumbled through the garage.

"Oh my God," she said with a giggle. "I haven't been this drunk since college."

"Careful," I said as she pitched forward.

I wrapped an arm around her middle to keep her from face-planting into the living room. Once she was steady on her feet, I gently released her, and she went tumbling anyway.

She lay sprawled on the floor, laughing. "Fuck, I am so fucking drunk."

"Can you get to bed?"

"Yep."

Then, she began to *crawl* across the hardwood floor in her dress. My eyes landed on her ass. Luckily, the material was flowy enough to cover her, but every inch of creamy thigh was on display, and if I were anyone else, I could have gotten a completely free show as she crawled on her hands and knees toward the back bedroom.

"Fuck," I growled under my breath.

"I'm going to have bruises," she said, flopping back down and rolling onto her back. "Someone is going to think I've been sucking cock."

I closed my eyes. Fuck, her filthy, drunk mouth was turning me on. And I needed to get that under control.

"Can I help you?"

"Suck cock?" she asked, her eyes wide and thoughtful.

I nearly choked. "To your bed."

"You want to get in bed with me?"

"I..." Jesus fucking Christ.

"I thought my brothers said look, but don't touch." I gaped at her as she was sprawled out on the floor, her arms stretched over her head. "Did you get a good enough look?"

"Nora," I groaned.

Where the hell had this come from? Thank fuck I'd gotten her out of the bar when I did. The shy girl who was awkward around guys turned into a sex kitten when drunk. I was never going to be able to scrub this image of her out of my mind.

"Please let me help you to bed."

She nodded and held her hand out. I pulled her to her feet, and when she stumbled again, I gave up, scooping her in my arms. Her head lolled against my shoulder as I walked down the hallway.

"I think I had one too many," she whispered.

"Yeah. Maybe so. I didn't realize you had no tolerance."

"Tamara tried to up my tolerance one summer in college, but all that meant was, I got drunk all summer long. It never did anything," she admitted.

"Let's not think about her. You did good tonight. We'll try to drink less next time."

She settled into my arms and said nothing.

I toed open her bedroom door. The room was spotless with just as many plants as the living room. I hadn't been in here. It was her private sanctuary. I could see her eye for design in every aspect of the place—from the wood bed to the fluffy white comforter and pillows to the shaggy brown-and-pink rug.

I lowered her gently onto the bed, the mattress dipping inward as her weight sank into it. "There you are."

She looked up at me with those starry-blue eyes. I hadn't realized when I set her down how close we were. I was still leaning over her. Our breaths mingled in the space. Part of me wished that I were drunk enough to give in to that look right there. I could claim her lips, pull her lush body against mine, and teach that dirty mouth all the ways I could make it moan.

"West," she whispered, "I had a good time."

I swallowed. "Me too."

She reached forward, brushing back my hair from my eyes. "Are you going to cut your hair?"

"I haven't decided. Should I?"

"I like it both ways," she said, dragging her hand down my cheek.

She drew me in closer. So close. I breathed in the Tiffany's perfume she sprayed on herself every morning. Our lips nearly touched. I could practically taste the honey on her lips.

Then, her eyes widened a fraction, as if she, too, realized how close we were. Then, she burst into laughter.

I jerked backward and laughed, too. "Dear God, you're drunk."

"I really, really am. Oh my God." She ran a hand down her face. "You should get to bed. I probably won't even remember this in the morning."

I cleared my throat. "Get some sleep."

"Hey, West," she said as I got to my feet.

"Yeah?"

"Thanks for a good night. It was what I needed."

"Anytime," I told her.

Then, I hastened out of her bedroom. That had been fucking close. So close that her perfume still lingered on my shirt. I could smell her all over me. I pushed down my erection as I hurried down the hall to my room. I wasn't going to be able to sleep without taking care of this.

I'd be lying if I said I wasn't thinking about her crawling around on the ground, talking about sucking cock, as I came in the shower later.

8

NORA

"Have you heard anything from West?" Annie asked. She leaned against the table at the center of the Wright Vineyard barn. Annie was in residency as a doctor at the local hospital, and her fiancé, Jordan Wright, came over to peck her on the cheek.

"Any word?" Jordan asked.

"I just texted to ask," I told them both.

Today was Campbell's big surprise birthday party. We'd worked it all out that West would hang with him in the studio until we got everything set up, and then Blaire would drive him over. They had their reasons all straightened out, but I'd still barely had enough time to make the barn presentable.

My phone dinged.

On my way now. Blaire just came to get Campbell.

"Clock is on," I called. "Fifteen minutes. Everyone to your positions."

Annie hopped up and grabbed her two best friends, Jennifer and Sutton. Jennifer was the photographer for the winery, and I worked with her regularly for my weddings. Sutton Wright had been Annie's bestie since high school, but we saw a lot less of her since she had two kids—Jason and Madison. Mostly because Madison was a walking tornado.

Piper strode over to the table with her sister, Peyton, and her newest roommate, Eve Houston. Eve was a big reason that Piper's winery had been saved. She was friends with Hollin and had joined our rec soccer team, The Tacos. She had a man-stealer reputation that the lot of us thought was ridiculous. And even though she'd been living with Piper and Blaire for a while now, she was still hesitant around us, as if expecting all of this to be a dream. We always told her we didn't deal with the bull-shit slut-shaming, and I hoped one day, she'd feel like she fit in.

Peyton grabbed my hand. "This is incredible. You've done a great job."

"Thank you."

It was so wonderful, having Peyton in town. She'd married Annie's brother, Isaac, last year when she returned from New York City to take over the Lubbock Ballet Company.

"I have news, too, before Campbell gets here," Peyton announced to the girls.

Piper and Annie grinned. They apparently already knew.

"I'm pregnant!"

All of us careened forward, pulling her into a hug and issuing our congratulations.

"It's a girl. We're calling her Autumn," she announced.

"Aly and Autumn," Jennifer said. Aly was Isaac's seven-year-old daughter from his first marriage. "Perfect."

"I love the name!" I gushed.

"Thank you," Peyton said. "I didn't want to over-shadow Campbell's surprise, but I have all of you here."

"We're so happy for you!" Annie said, giving her a crushing hug. "I can't wait to have another niece."

We all gushed over Peyton for a few more minutes. Then, the door to the barn burst open. Everyone froze, as if anticipating Campbell even though my alarm said we had three more minutes.

Instead, Weston Wright strode into the barn.

"He's right behind me," he announced.

My heart galloped at the sight of him. We hadn't talked about what had happened at the bar last night. Or how drunk and horny I'd been when we got back. I remembered enough of the interaction to be embarrassed at the thought of it all. Had I crawled on my hands and knees and made blow-job jokes? Had we almost kissed? That still felt fuzzy in my mind. That couldn't be right. Weston had made it clear that he wasn't interested in me. My own behavior was cringeworthy, considering that fact.

I'd had a crush on him when we moved in together. We were strangers then, and he was the hot guy who had taken me in when I needed a place to live. He saw me through the worst of what had happened with August.

He got me ice cream that time I ran into August at Starbucks. He stayed for our soccer game the day we had to play August's new team. And a million other littler interactions that made me wonder if this could possibly go somewhere or if I was insane.

And then he'd gone. All of that pulled apart. But now, he was back, and was I crazy for thinking of him like this? He was probably going back to LA, just like Campbell. I didn't have a job like Blaire, where I could pick up and leave anytime I wanted.

But still...

But still...

"You ready?" West asked when he reached me.

I cleared my throat and nodded. "Yep. All set. He still doesn't know?"

"No, but he's irritated," he said with a chuckle. "He thinks we're going out to eat and is confused why he has to pick you up from here."

"Can't blame him," I said with a smile. "All right, everyone. Get into position. He'll be here any minute."

I pointed at Hollin, who cut the lights. We all hid behind the table at the back of the barn. A white tablecloth had been draped across the front, so none of us were visible. We'd practiced to make sure that Campbell wouldn't be able to see us.

Weston pulled in tight next to me so that we were shoulder to shoulder. There was only enough light to see his big blue eyes. He squeezed my knee gently and shot me a wink. I was glad that he couldn't see more than that because my cheeks flared red.

Then, the door to the barn creaked open again.

Blaire's voice filtered through the opening. "It'll just be a minute. Come on."

Campbell grumbled something low, and then he was inside.

Hollin flipped the lights, and we all jumped up, yelling, "Happy birthday!"

Campbell's face went from irritated to dismayed to a forced rockstar smile. "Wow," he said, blinking into the lights. His eyes went to Blaire, who was smiling brightly. "You did this?"

"We all did."

Then, he kissed her, and we all cheered a second time.

Music came on, and everyone moved onto the dance floor. Campbell walked around the room, thanking everyone for coming. When he finally landed on me and Weston, his smile dropped.

He punched West in the shoulder. "You motherfucker."

West laughed and rubbed his shoulder. "You're welcome."

"Hey, ass, it was Hollin's idea," I said with a grin.

"What are you accusing me of?" Hollin asked. He pulled our brother into a hug.

Campbell rolled his eyes. "You decided on this party?"

"Me and Nora did. Aren't you so excited?"

Campbell snorted. "Y'all are all assholes."

"You know he's in a mood when he pulls out the *y'all*s," Blaire said.

Weston punched him back. "You should let us do this

shit more often. Why are you so against surprises anyway?"

"I'm not," Campbell lied.

Hollin and I shared a private smile. Campbell glared at both of us.

"Don't fucking say it," Campbell warned.

Hollin grinned devilishly. "What? About the clown at your twelfth birthday that scared you shitless?"

"The time you ran out of the house, screaming, when it jumped out at you?" I added.

Campbell looked to the ceiling. "Thank God I have siblings."

Weston cracked up. "Oh man, I need this story in its entirety."

"Not a chance," Campbell growled.

Blaire shook her head. "Tell me about it later."

"About what?" Julian asked, stepping up to our party. His brother, Jordan, at his side.

"Something about a clown?" Jordan asked.

I was lucky to have my cousins in Lubbock. Jordan and Julian were related to West on his dad's side, but their mom was my aunt. So even though we were both related to them, we weren't related to each other. And since Jordan and Julian had lived in Vancouver through my childhood, I'd never gotten to know them. But with them here and Jordan now engaged to Annie and Julian living with Jennifer, I knew they were here to stay. My family had shattered after my mom died, but it was starting to stitch back together after all these years.

"Fuck both of you," Campbell said to me and Hollin.

We just hit knuckles. Ganging up on Campbell was half the fun.

The rest of the party dispersed as Campbell turned his attention to our cousins. I was left alone with West, and I knew this was the moment I should take.

Our eyes met. "Hey."

"The party turned out great."

"Thanks," I said, on steady ground when talking about work. Though I knew I couldn't let last night stand.

West had been gone this morning when I woke up. He'd left Gatorade, Tylenol, and a note that said, *Hope you feel okay. Heading to the gym. —West*. It was thought-ful, but I was sure it was also a way to avoid the awkward-ness to follow.

"Sorry about last night," I forced out.

"Sorry?"

"You know, about...getting super drunk and every-thing that happened afterward."

He laughed and ran a hand back through his floppy, dark hair. "You don't have anything to be sorry for, Nor."

"You sure? I remember a very embarrassing almost kiss, where I then started laughing at how drunk I was."

He grinned. Not at all miffed by that. "You remember that, huh?"

My cheeks heated. "I do."

"Look, it was good to see you cut loose. You should do it more often."

"It was nice to not *think* for once. Though I felt pretty dumb when I woke up."

"I liked seeing you that way," he admitted.

Something heated in my core at those words. He'd

liked the loose, flirty, almost-*sexy* Nora Abbey. I'd liked her, too. I wished I could find her right now.

"Maybe we should do it again. I'll be in the studio all week with Campbell—because he's a workaholic—but maybe next weekend?"

"Sure." I bit my lip. "I'd like that."

"Good. It's a date."

I swallowed at that word. *Date.* A date with Weston Wright. Even if it definitely, absolutely, for sure was *not* a real date with Weston Wright.

9

NORA

True to his word, I barely saw Weston the rest of the week. He would come back in the evenings, guzzle water, and promptly pass out. He'd mentioned something about what he and Campbell were working on in the studio, but it was technical, and all these years with my rockstar brother hadn't equipped me to understand. I'd thought the album was done. But there was a lot more that went into it when perfectionists like Campbell and West were working on it.

"Hey," West said as he strode into the house, still holding his guitar.

"Hey, you got back early."

"Blaire got irritated that Campbell's home and spending every waking second on a new song even though the album is supposed to be done."

I laughed. "That sounds right. Is the song good?"

"Yeah. Honestly, it's absolutely necessary. We just didn't know we were missing it."

He tipped his head to the side, and I followed him

into the bedroom between our two rooms. It had been converted into a music room with guitars, keyboards, an upright piano, and every other type of instrument I could name. Weston played all of them, including harmonica, saxophone, and trumpet. I had no idea how he could play them all.

He set the guitar into its position and sank down at the keyboard. I knew the piano would always be his favorite. He started to sketch out a melody. "What do you think of this?"

"Is this the new song?"

He shook his head. "Just something I've been working on."

"I like it." It was soft and lilting, strung together on a series of high notes. It drifted and spiraled and came back to the same tune again. "It's beautiful. Doesn't sound like Cosmere though."

"No. Not for them." His fingers continued as he stared up at me. My stomach flipped at that look. He was off in his own music dream world, and somehow, I'd been pulled into it like a tornado. My face heated at the connection. Then, abruptly, he stopped and looked away. "Something else."

"Well, it's good."

"It was always my dream to play keys. I wanted to headline on them but realized quickly that it was impossible. Getting to do this with Campbell," he said wistfully as he shook his head, "it's a dream come true. Feels like everything is in my grasp finally."

"You've earned it."

He shrugged. "Just happy to be along for the ride." He looked me up and down. "Are we still on for tonight?"

I tucked a strand of hair behind my ear. "I'm up for it if you are."

"You bet, Snickers."

My stomach fluttered at the ridiculous nickname. "I have no idea what to wear."

"I can help."

"Really?"

"Sure. Try on the options for me."

"Okay," I agreed. We'd decided on a cocktail bar, and I felt clueless.

"Last time was to get your feet wet. Practicing on frat bros and such in that bar was easy enough, but they're not the kind of guy you want to date. You can use the same moves on people you would actually go on a date with."

"Right. That makes sense." I stared down at my sweats and laughed. "Probably not this then."

"Probably not."

"Give me a minute," I told him.

I headed into my room. I had plenty of nice dresses. I wore a lot of them when I was working weddings, but I wanted something with a wow factor. Something that would make me get noticed. I'd spent so long in the shadows that I didn't know how to look in my closet and pick something to get attention.

I grabbed a short black dress from the back and slid it over my curvy frame. I had more shoes than anything in the closet, and I settled on a pair of booties.

I strutted back down the hallway and found Weston

still at the piano, notating the song onto sheet music. I cleared my throat. He turned around and went perfectly still. His eyes crawled down the length of my dress—from my exposed cleavage to my bare thighs.

He nearly choked. "You look great, but maybe something with color."

My body heated from the way he'd seemed barely able to get the words out. So, maybe Weston Wright wasn't completely impervious to me.

With that in mind, I returned to my closet and slid on a royal-blue dress that I'd worn out with Tamara once and promptly never wore again because it was way too short and tight. I had a feeling he was going to veto this one. I knew I looked hot and was interested to see if I got the same reaction.

"Well?" I asked, doing a small twirl for him.

His jaw clenched, and then he slowly released a breath. But I didn't miss the way he took me in from top to bottom, as if he were about to devour me whole.

"Not that one," he managed to get out.

A small smile of triumph rippled through me. Well, well, well, maybe I wasn't just his best friend's little sister.

I returned to my room, reached farther back in my closet, and grabbed a red dress with a flowy skirt that I'd never worn. I always felt like it was a little too showy for weddings, which was where I wore most of my cocktail attire, but it felt just right for this. I grabbed black heels with little buckles across the top that made my short legs look so much longer.

"That one," Weston said as soon as I entered the

music room. He coughed into his hand and then nodded. "Yep, that one."

I did a twirl for him, the layers of the skirt floating upward as I did so. "You like it?"

"I love it," he muttered.

"All right. I'll do my hair and makeup, and then we can go."

———

An hour later, I slid the dress back onto my body and came out to find Weston already waiting for me. My jaw dropped, and I hastily recovered.

Weston Wright was dressed up in a white button-up, black dress slacks, a thick black belt, and dress shoes. I could hardly believe it. He was the perpetual *ripped jeans and T-shirt* guy. He drove a Subaru with over a hundred thousand miles. He let his hair grow out until it bothered him before a haircut. I hadn't expected him to even own a suit. Let alone be able to fill it like a fucking god.

"Wow, West," I muttered.

He grinned. "Figured if you were dressing nice, I should make an effort."

"This is a little more than an effort."

He held out the tie that he hadn't yet tied around his neck. The white button-up was undone to the second button, and personally, I was a fan. "Still not used to this thing though."

I slid the material between my fingers, dragging it out of his hand. "Eh, you don't need it."

"Well, that's decided."

His eyes traveled to where I now held his tie. Part of me wanted to say fuck the pretense and kiss him. He might find me attractive, but that didn't mean he wanted to kiss me. It didn't mean he wanted to complicate our roommate situation or betray Campbell. He felt a great obligation to my older brother, and I doubted he'd do anything to jeopardize their friendship.

So, I tossed the tie to the couch and smiled brilliantly up at him. This was my flirt coach. That was all it was. "Round two?"

He nodded. "Let's go."

We got into the Subaru and headed away from the house. When he veered away from downtown, I looked at him in confusion. "Where exactly are we going?"

"You don't actually want to date frat bros. So, we're going to need higher-end clientele."

"And where would that be in Lubbock, Texas?" I asked skeptically. I'd dressed the part, but I hadn't considered that we had nice enough bars for me to practice in.

"Manhattan 9."

"I haven't heard of it. How do *you* know about it?"

"Well, it's a speakeasy, and they have live music on the weekends. I played piano there a few times when I first moved into town."

"What? You didn't tell me that."

He shrugged. "It was sort of an escape. It was hard when I first moved here and Whitt and Harley were still in Seattle."

I nodded in understanding. "So, I'm trying to get a guy to ask for my number again?"

"No, we're past that. You were a natural, as I'd suspected."

I laughed. "I was far from a natural."

"Either way, you excelled. Did that guy call you after all?"

"Well, yeah."

"Exactly. So, tonight, you're going to try to meet a guy you can see yourself agreeing to go on a date with when he inevitably calls you. More than a drink or a phone number. If you hit it off, then you'll spend the night hanging with him at the bar."

I gulped. "That's a big ask."

"You'll do fine."

"What if he wants to go back to his place?"

Weston stiffened. "Look, only you can answer that question. If you want to go home with him, that's on you." His eyes cut to mine. "Do you have a condom?"

I sat frozen in place at that question. "What? No! That's...that's way too soon."

He released a breath. "Well, that's your answer then."

"I mean, Jesus, I've only ever been with one guy."

Weston arched an eyebrow. "Really?"

"I mean, yeah. I've only dated one, only slept with one. That's the whole point of all of this."

"Those things don't always mean the same thing."

My cheeks colored. "They do for me."

"Nothing to be ashamed of," he insisted. "Only do what you're comfortable with tonight. Just try to have fun and don't think too much."

Easier said than done.

10

WESTON

Nora struck out the first hour, but when she was finishing up her first drink, she started talking to a new guy. I knew it was the one she was going to practice on based solely on the fact that her shoulders were no longer up to her ears. She almost looked relaxed.

I clenched my jaw.

This was what I'd wanted. This was what we'd planned for. This was the entire reason we were here.

I knew the owner of the speakeasy. I knew the bartenders were trained to spot anyone suspicious. They looked out for girls who were there and were fastidious about safety. That was why I'd thought it would be an okay place to start. The kind of guy who would come here was leagues different than the idiots we'd first started with.

But somehow, now that she was talking to a guy in a suit and tie with his blond hair spiked in the front and a million-dollar smile, it all became real. And I didn't like it.

"You look like you could use this," the bartender said, sliding a shot toward me.

"Thanks, Layla," I said with a nod.

Layla had been working here for a few years. We'd become friends in those first few months when I came to the city and played the keys in here to pass the time.

"So, who's the girl?"

"My roommate."

She grimaced. "Rough, man."

"Yeah." I shrugged. "Do you know the guy she's talking to?"

"Bryan something," she said with a nod. "He's in here a lot. Tips well."

The important thing.

"You going to watch her talk to other guys all night?"

I was. That was the plan at least.

I hadn't considered how frustrated I'd get by the process. This was what I should be doing. It was the right thing to do. I was helping her get over August. Bringing her out of her shell. And it wasn't like we could do anything. I still couldn't stop the beat racketing through my chest.

"I guess I am," I told her.

"Well, drinks on me then. You're a good guy, West."

A good guy. That was who I'd always been. Until those six months in LA when I'd let loose with the band. I could spin Nora Abbey so hard if I wanted to. I could break all the rules and have her in my arms by the end of the night. But I wasn't that guy. I didn't want to be that guy.

Even if the way she'd looked, twirling around in her

little dresses, made me think all sorts of filthy thoughts about her. Had she known she was driving me insane with every spin? Fuck.

Nora flashed the guy another smile. They'd been talking for a half hour. Jesus Christ, I didn't want to sit here and watch this.

I messed around on my phone, texting with Whitt for a while until, suddenly, Nora was standing before me again.

I breathed a sigh of relief. It must have fallen apart somewhere. We could work on it a different night.

"Hey," she said buoyantly.

"How's it going?"

She grinned. "Good. You were right. This is easier than I thought."

"Oh really?" My eyes drifted back to where Bryan something was seated with a group of his friends. He was looking right at us. He didn't seem particularly pleased that she was now talking to me.

"Yeah. I already knew Bryan. He and I had a class together at Tech my senior year. I'd completely forgotten about it until he mentioned it."

Her senior year. Which meant she'd been with August. Made sense that she hadn't noticed the guy, but that he'd noticed her.

"Plus, you see the redhead? That's Jana. She used to run tours at Wright Vineyard for a while."

With Tamara was implied but not said.

"Well, that's good."

"And they—well, Bryan, asked if I wanted to hop to

Funky Door with them for cocktails." She did a little jig, like she'd won the lottery. "That's good, right?"

"It is. You still planning to come home tonight?"

Her eyes flicked back to Bryan's. He smiled brilliantly at her.

"Definitely. I'm not...well, you know." She flushed. "Anyway, you don't have to follow us."

"Are you sure?"

"Yeah. I'll practice the rest of the night. That's what I'm supposed to be doing, right?"

I nodded. Even though I wanted to tell her there was no fucking way that she was going to a different bar with this douche. But I'd set her on this path. It would be crazy for me to do that now.

"It is, but are you sure that you feel safe with them?"

"Yeah. Totally. Maybe I wouldn't with just Bryan, but I know Jana."

"Okay. But call me if you need anything. Anything at all."

She nodded. "I will. Thanks for the help, West. I never would have done this without you."

And as she scampered off, I tried to relax. This was what she needed. It was the right thing to do. She should have the space she needed to date other people after what August had done to her. It was my own fault for not realizing that spending all this time with her, seeing her in every sense of the word, would change how I felt.

I'd been into her when we moved in together, but a healthy fear of her brothers had kept me at bay. Not to mention, she had been in deep mourning over her last relationship. She was still recovering from that, of course. But she was finally starting to come into her own.

Layla pushed another shot my way.

I shoved it back across the bar. "Thanks, but I'm good."

"If you say so." Layla's eyes trailed Nora as she headed out of the bar. "You said she's going to Funky Door? I know the bar manager there. I can have them watch out for her."

I breathed another sigh of relief. "I'd appreciate that."

I passed her some cash and left. I watched Nora get into the back of a shiny yellow sports car next to Jana. Bryan was driving. He shot me a shit-eating grin as he slammed the door and pulled away.

Fuck.

The sight of Bryan's smug smile made me want to put my fist through his fucking face. He wasn't getting any tonight, but he thought that he'd stolen her away from me. And he was pleased by it.

I ran a hand down my face. This was so fucked up. I couldn't fall for Campbell's little sister. She was off-limits.

I stomped to my car in irritation. This was supposed to be simple. How come it was never fucking simple?

My phone rang as I was driving home, and I put Whitt on speaker. "Hey."

"So, how'd it go?"

"Why do you care? Don't you think it's a bad idea?"

My twin laughed. "You have a lot of bad ideas. Helping out your roommate get some ass is probably the dumbest."

"I'm not trying to help her get laid," I grumbled. "I just want her to get over her ex."

"The best way to get over someone…"

"Is to get under someone else. Yeah, I know."

"And you're still not admitting that you wouldn't mind being that guy?"

"Campbell would *kill* me," I snarled.

"If he found out."

I laughed hoarsely. "My brother, the rule follower, is telling me to break the rules."

"Every rule follower knows when to break the rules to their advantage."

"Nah," I said with a shake of my head. "I couldn't do that to Nora. Let alone fuck things up with Campbell. Could you imagine if he found out I'd slept with his sister? He's given me everything."

"That's fair," Whitton agreed. "Then, you should find some other local girl to channel your energy into, so you stop thinking about your off-limits roommate."

I huffed. "Yeah, sure. Like Eve?"

Whitt went silent for a few seconds. "How the hell did you know?"

"I'm your twin brother, asshole."

I'd noticed them talking briefly at Campbell's party. I hadn't said anything then because I knew Whitt would automatically go on the defensive. As he was right now.

"She doesn't seem interested," Whitt said flatly. "But I see how you pivoted this to be about me. When you're the one pining after Nora."

I groaned. "I am not *pining*."

"You should hope that she fucks that guy tonight, so

you can move on already and not screw everything up that you've worked for. If LA is your dream, then doing anything to jeopardize that would be stupid, even for you."

"Thanks, Whitt," I muttered. "Always so helpful."

Thinking of Nora fucking someone else tonight made me see red. I was glad that I'd already pulled into the garage and killed the engine. It didn't help that every word he'd uttered was true.

I couldn't have Nora Abbey.

And I needed to forget about her.

11

NORA

"Thanks for the ride, Jana," I said.

"Anytime. It was good seeing you out, girl. We should do it again!"

"Definitely."

I waved at her as she drove away. Apprehension still rippled through my gut. I should have called West. He'd said I could call him for anything. I should have stuffed down my pride and given him a call. But I felt like a failure and also like I wanted to kill Bryan. What a douche.

The house was dark on the inside and I blew out a breath. West must have gone to sleep already. It was only just after midnight. I'd planned to be there until bar close. If only Bryan had been as nice as he'd first appeared. This was the part of dating I hadn't been looking forward to. Why did a guy have to seem nice and then turn out to be a prick? Could save me all the time and trouble by revealing who they were at the beginning.

I stomped up the front walk and stuck the key into the

front door. The handle turned easily. He must have left it open for me. I closed the door behind me and kicked off my heels. I squeaked when I found Weston seated on the couch, the light from his phone illuminating his face.

"You're awake! Why are you sitting in here in the dark?"

"Couldn't sleep and decided to wait for you to get home." He checked the time. "It's early."

"Yeah, well, the night wasn't exactly a Disney movie."

Weston came to his feet, stretching to his full height. "How so?"

I shook my head. "It's stupid. I don't want to get into it."

"Nora?" he said, stopping me before I could escape. "What happened?"

"Nothing."

He raised his eyebrows. "Did he hurt you?"

"No. He just..." I sighed and crossed my arms. But he waited right there for an explanation. "He's friends with August."

Weston frowned. "Ah."

"Yeah. And I guess there was some kind of...bet." I rolled my eyes. "I can't even finish that sentence. Some of his so-called friends were trying to see who could bag me first."

"He *told* you about this?"

"Well, no. He pressured me to go home with him and didn't exactly take kindly to me saying no."

Weston's eyes went flinty. "I'll kill him."

I put my hand on his arm. "Just leave it. It's stupid. It's so fucking stupid and childish. Jana was the one who confessed to the bet. She'd thought they'd all forgotten about it since it'd happened right after the breakup. But I guess not."

"What a fucking douche bag."

"Yeah," I whispered.

"Why didn't you call me? I could have come to get you. I could have *handled* Bryan."

I waved him off. "I don't know. I wanted to be able to handle it myself. Jana drove me home." I bit my lip. "I should have called. I'm sorry."

"Hey, don't apologize to me," he said at once. "You have nothing to apologize for."

"I know. I just thought I'd succeeded at this next coaching session. And it turned out, I was someone's stupid bet," I ground out. "He felt entitled to sleep with me because he'd bought me a few drinks."

"Fuck," he growled. "No guy is entitled to anything from you, Nora. And any guy who believes he is, isn't the guy you want to sleep with. He'd end up being a selfish prick in bed."

I shrugged with a sigh. "Wouldn't matter anyway."

Weston tilted his head to the side. "What does that mean?"

"I'm difficult." The words came out on barely a breath. I couldn't even meet his gaze as I said them. I was so embarrassed by the admission.

"What does that mean?" West prodded.

But I didn't want to say it. I didn't want to confess this to him, too. I was broken up enough about what had happened tonight. At the fact that I even needed someone to teach me how to flirt or how to date. I should have known these things. It would be worse if he knew this about me, too.

"Nothing. Forget I mentioned it."

"Nora, you're not difficult," he said plainly. "That's bullshit language used by guys who are trying to control women. It's fucked up."

"Not...not difficult like that," I whispered.

"Then, what?"

"You know..." I looked up at him, begging for him to understand what I was saying. But he just stared back at me in confusion. "I don't...I don't orgasm with a guy. It's, like...impossible."

Weston stared at me for a few seconds, as if waiting for me to throw in a punch line. Because that couldn't possibly be what I'd just said. My cheeks flushed at that look.

"What?" he croaked.

"Forget it," I muttered.

"Do you come when you masturbate?"

My mouth opened and closed. My blush moving from my cheeks to my ears and neck. Mutely, I nodded.

"You're not difficult," he insisted. "That's not true."

"It really is. It's never happened...and August said..."

Weston took a step forward. "What did he say?"

I swallowed. "Just that..." Fuck, I'd never told anyone this. "That it was normal for girls to not get off."

"And did he suggest you still had to get *him* off?" West almost growled.

I glanced down with a shrug. "Yeah, I mean..."

West looked as if he could barely hold himself back as

he entered my personal space. I tilted my head up to look at him. Without my heels on, he towered over me.

"Listen to me, everything he told you is a lie. *A lie*." Weston held my gaze firm and steady. "I can show you that he's wrong."

The words left me stunned. Show me. He could *show me*.

"How?" I whispered.

I'd had a few drinks. I was a little tipsy. Enough to ask that one word that destroyed any semblance of control I had. But not drunk enough to be incoherent.

"We can call it a teachable moment," he said calmly. "I've taught you about everything else. You trust me, right?"

I nodded.

"Then, I can show you that what he said is wrong. If you want me to do that."

A pregnant pause followed his words. My core tightened at the thought of what that could possibly mean. What he was offering. I wanted it. I wanted it so bad. I hadn't been touched in ten long months. My body ached for him to prove to me how wrong August had been about my body. And he was so damn confident about it. Like I'd been led, blindfolded, for most of my life.

I was ready to remove it.

"Okay," I said breathily.

"It doesn't have to involve feelings," he said automatically, as if he had to talk me into this.

"No feelings," I agreed.

Except there was already something brewing between

us. Something that I couldn't quite put my finger on. But I couldn't deny it any more than I could stop breathing.

"You're sure?"

I nodded because I couldn't say another word with him so close to me, breathing the same air, my heart constricting almost painfully so. He took my hand and drew me back to the couch. I took a seat next to him. I clenched my hand into a fist to keep from shaking with anticipation.

"Okay. I'm not going to kiss you. I'm only going to touch you here," he said, gesturing between my legs. "You can tell me to stop at any time. Do you understand?"

My eyes met his, and I shivered at the look of lust reflected back at me. "Yes."

But I wanted him to kiss me. God, I fucking wanted him to kiss me. I wanted to lean in right now and claim those supple lips for my own. I wanted to offer myself up to him on a silver platter. No matter that I'd only ever been with one guy. I never felt like Weston would hurt me. He'd only ever put my own interests first.

I jumped at the first contact against my thigh. "Sorry," I whispered.

He smiled back at me. "No apologizing."

I gulped and nodded as his hand slid up my skirt. At the first touch of him against the lace of my thong, I jumped again. I bit back another apology. He hesitated a second, looking into my gaze, waiting for me to tell him to stop. I had no intention of doing so.

He stroked me gently through my underwear, and I squirmed at the heat that built there. His other hand came to my knee. The feel of his hand against me nearly made me groan.

"Open," he commanded. Then, he spread my legs, inch by inch, baring me before him until I was wide open. "Better."

I nearly fell apart right then and there. Not orgasming —because that had never happened—but collapsing with desire. Weston Wright was commanding my body, and I was letting him.

His fingers skimmed the top of my underwear. "I'm going to touch you now."

I bit my lip as he did just that. Those callous fingers skimming over the light hair until he reached my clit. I bucked against his fingers at the first gentle brush.

His voice was hoarse when he said, "Look at me."

My eyes had been squeezed shut, but I forced them open. I looked into his beautiful face as he moved two fingers between the lips of my pussy and found the slickness there, waiting for him.

His eyes flickered wider when he discovered how wet I was from him. He looked like he was going to say something about it, but he just moved those two fingers through the wetness until he reached my opening.

"I'm going to finger you," he said, our eyes still locked.

It should have been less hot with him telling me everything before it happened, but somehow, it only heightened every move. I bit my lip harder, waiting. But then I realized he wanted me to say it was okay.

The only word that came out was, "Please."

He swallowed hard. Then, he thrust forward, inserting one finger inside of me. I couldn't look at him any longer. I tipped my head backward and arched against the couch.

Oh God, oh God, oh God!

"How does that feel?" he asked, voice strained.

"Good," I groaned.

Then, a second finger joined it, stretching me easily.

"And this?"

"Uh," I gasped. "Fuck."

He started a slow, steady rhythm, in and out. In and out. I could feel my body coiling in on itself. The tempo dragging me closer to the edge. All of the pent-up energy I'd been holding on to coalescing into something primal in my core.

Then, his thumb joined the mix. He slicked it through my wetness and then circled it slowly—so fucking slowly —against my clit. I couldn't help it; I gasped. My legs shamelessly fell farther apart. I wanted more. I would give him anything at this point. He had to know it, too, because I could feel his own breathing matching mine.

"Are you close?" he asked.

His thumb circled faster and harder. Just like how I did it when I was alone in my room. Only this was Weston's hand, his thumb, and I had no idea what the fuck he was going to do next.

"I...I..."

He curled his fingers up inside of me as he dragged them in and out. And something about that motion and the faster tempo and him working my clit made everything go fuzzy at the edges. I couldn't breathe. I couldn't think. I could barely function at all.

"Come for me," he whispered hoarsely against my ear.

And I was already there. So close. That, at the filthy words, I broke apart. Everything snapped, and I shuddered, my pussy contracting against his fingers over and over, as if trying to keep him from releasing me.

I made incoherent sounds of pleasure as the climax hit me. And then when I finally came down, I cracked my eyes open and looked at him with sex eyes, my chest heaving from the exertion.

"West," I whispered.

He slowly withdrew his hand from my underwear—he hadn't even needed to remove it. My eyes drifted to the sweats he had on. His erection was jutting upward, and he pressed his hand against it to cover it. As if he didn't even want me to see what my orgasm had done to him.

"There," he said. "You're not difficult at all."

He shot me a small smile and then disappeared into his room, leaving me in a puddle of goo and a swirl of confusion.

12

WESTON

I couldn't escape fast enough.

I stumbled into my room, slamming the door closed. My chest rose fast and hard, aching. My heavy pants were barely controlled. I had no idea how the fuck I'd been able to keep it together.

Truly, I couldn't believe I'd even gone there with her.

Sure, I'd made up some excuse, but I hadn't thought that she'd agree. My brain had just short-circuited at the words coming out of her mouth. That August had fucked her up bad enough to think that she couldn't orgasm. Not that he hadn't wanted to spend the time getting to know her body and do the work to get her there.

I couldn't see straight.

I'd just wanted to get her off. Right then and there.

Forget the conversation I'd had with Whitt where I'd decided to let her go. That had fucked everything up. No way could I let it stand.

Then, she'd come all over my fingers, her face open and flush with desire after the orgasm. It had taken everything in me not to flip her over and bury my cock balls deep into her.

I'd gotten her worked up. I'd wanted to finish what I'd started.

But I couldn't.

A teachable fucking moment.

Holy fuck. What a load of shit.

And she'd not only gone along with it; she'd practically been eager. Her body had responded like a fucking instrument as I plucked the chords. The sounds of her coming had been the chorus to a beautiful fucking song.

I still had the smell of her on my fingers. The sound of her orgasm in my ears. The heat of her skin against my palm.

Fucking fuck, fuck. I was screwed. How did I come back from this?

I palmed my erection through the material of my sweatpants. I'd thrown them on with loose boxers when I got home. Big mistake. I was hard as a rock, and she would have to be blind to not have seen it. Fuck. God, I needed to do something about this. A cold shower. Yes, that was what I needed.

I burst into the bathroom, cursing myself for giving her the room with the en suite bathroom. I had to slink back down the hall and inside. Luckily, I didn't run into her before I got inside, turned the water on, and shucked off my clothes.

My body was still hyped from getting her off. I couldn't get her out of my head. The way she'd responded so easily to all my commands. The first touch of me slicking my way through her folds. How she'd already been wet just from me touching her.

I groaned. "Fuck it."

I switched the water to boiling, and when it was ready, I got inside and let the hot water cascade down my back. I was utterly fucked. I was never going to be able to get her out of my system. I'd thought it was bad when she was crawling around on the ground, talking about sucking cock. Now that I'd gotten her to come, there was no hope.

"Fucking fuck."

With a sigh of relief, I palmed my cock in my hand. I shouldn't jack off. I didn't deserve to feel anything after this. I needed to escape her. And yet I couldn't. I was already regretting that I was washing the smell of her from my hand.

I wasn't gentle as I jerked my cock up and down. I tugged on it forcefully, achingly. I wanted the torment as I imagined what it would feel like if this was her pussy instead of my hand. God, even if it was just her wet mouth around me.

She'd mentioned sucking cock. I could fill her right up, grab her hair, thrust into her mouth like I owned it. I could own her. Every inch of her. Every hole. It was a torment to even think about how she'd react to taking my cock in her mouth.

I slammed a hand against the shower wall, feeling the first prick of orgasm up my spine. I was close. Of course I was fucking close. I'd never come in my pants, just from fingering her.

But if it were her pussy. Dear fucking God. She'd been so fucking tight. So fucking wet. I could spread her lips and sink inch after inch into her, take what I wanted so badly.

I came in long spurts to the image of her coming on my fingers. I coated the glossy white shower wall with my come until I was fully spent. Then, I bent forward at the waist, breathing harshly.

"Fuck," I groaned again.

I was fucked.

After a few minutes of recovery, I cleaned up my mess, turned off the shower, and threw a towel low around my hips. I didn't even bother drying off. I needed to get back to the safety of my room so that I could escape the image of her. I didn't trust myself to not demand more from her.

I cracked the bathroom door open at the same moment her bedroom door opened. She made a small squeak as her eyes widened, dragging down my mostly naked and soaking wet body. Her nostrils flared, and her grip tightened on the doorknob.

"I was...just getting some water," she said.

She'd also taken a shower. Her makeup was gone, and her long blonde bob had darkened to brown and dragged past her collarbone from the water. She'd changed into a blue tank top and sleeping pants. A rivulet of water ran down between her chest, pooling between her breasts. I watched the water, jealous of its trajectory.

"Did you need anything?" she asked me.

I clenched my jaw. I couldn't tell her what I needed from her. Because what I wanted, she wasn't ready to give. And I shouldn't have even taken what I had.

"I'm good," I lied.

She nodded. "Okay then." She took a few steps down the hall. A few steps closer to me.

I still hadn't moved. I didn't trust myself to move.

Then, she smiled a small, shy thing at me. "Good night, West. Sweet dreams."

Oh, I was going to have dreams. But they weren't going to be anything but sweet torture.

"Night, Snickers."

She disappeared into the kitchen, and I hurried back to my room, closing the door for the night on all of my temptations, just a few feet away.

PART III

FINE LINE

13

NORA

Weston fucking Wright had fingerbanged me in the living room in the name of science.

Nothing made sense anymore.

It was a few days later, and still, it was all I could think about. Not Annie and Jordan's wedding, which was only two weeks away. Or the Locke-King wedding that I was planning for next month. Not anything at all while I was in my office at Wright Vineyard, trying against all hope to be productive.

Except all I could think about was the sensation of his fucking fingers on my clit. The way he'd made me come harder than I ever had with my *own* fingers. And he hadn't even taken my panties off.

All those years of assuming I couldn't come, of being expressly told that I probably couldn't, and he'd done it in a matter of minutes. My brain was in a fog from it.

I'd faked getting my glass of water so that I could see him again. And then I was the one salivating over the fact that he was in nothing but a towel around his hips. Shirtless and dripping wet, and suddenly, *I* was the one who was wet again. While he seemed completely unaffected by what had happened one room over.

I got my water and lay in bed, wondering what the fuck had just happened. And what I was supposed to do with the knowledge that my roommate could finger-fuck an orgasm out of me like it was his job. What would it be like with his cock? Which was only two rooms away.

It had been nearly impossible to sleep.

Then, the next morning, he'd acted as if nothing had changed. I'd had to play along despite getting way less sleep than necessary and having to book it to Starbucks to survive the rest of the day.

This was the point where I wished I had my best friend to work out what to do from here. But of course, Tamara was the problem, not the solution.

A knock on my office door pulled me from my thoughts.

"Come in."

And to my surprise, Eve Houston opened the door. "Hey, Nora."

I stood in surprise. "Hey, Eve."

Even though Eve was only a year older than me, I always felt so young in her presence. As if she was so much more worldly than I'd ever be. I didn't know if it was because I'd only had one boyfriend and she'd dated beyond my wildest dreams. Or if it was her self-confident poise, the assured tilt to her chin, the knowledge in those emerald-green eyes.

"Mind if I come in?"

"Of course." I gestured to the seat in front of me. "Feel free."

She slid inside, pacing into the room in tattered black jeans and a slinky black silk top. She dropped unceremoniously into the chair and crossed her feet, revealing the platform Doc Martens. She swept her long black hair over her shoulder and pursed her lips. "I hope this is an okay time."

"Totally fine. I was just..." I trailed off as I stared at my blank screen. Nothing. I'd been doing nothing. "What can I help you with? Do you have an upcoming event?"

Eve laughed softly. "Uh, no. I'm not a big planner. And, yeah, no weddings forthcoming." She twirled an emerald band on her right ring finger. "It's not about that."

"Okay?" I couldn't help it coming out as a question.

Eve and I both played on The Tacos soccer team. She'd replaced August as one of our forwards, and objectively, she was better than he was. So, I saw her every week on the pitch and when I hung out with Piper and Blaire, but we'd never had a one-on-one. If I was honest, I'd always been a little intimidated by her.

"So...you live with Weston Wright, right?"

My stomach dropped out of my body. Fear replaced anything else I'd been feeling prior. Was she...into West? Because if that was the case, I was utterly fucked. There was no way I could compete with someone like Eve Houston.

"Uh, yeah. Yeah, we're roommates."

"He's pretty cool, right?"

I nodded mutely. My hands clenched into fists in my lap. Fuck, this was going to suck. "Yep."

"He's here for good? I mean...his brother and sister moved here and everything."

I gulped. "Uh, yeah. As far as I know. Harley is at Tech on scholarship, and Whitt followed her here. But, yeah, West came first." I tried for a small laugh. "Are you wanting to date West?"

Eve tilted her head to the side and looked at me. I clearly did not manage casual. Even to myself, my voice had come out strained.

"Uh, no. That wasn't what I was asking at all. Though did I miss that y'all are dating?" she asked carefully.

"No!" I said quickly. "Uh, no. We're not dating."

Eve arched an eyebrow. "That was a bit defensive, eh? You're going to have to try that a couple more times before someone believes you. Trust me. Neutral expressions and responses are better when you have a secret. This is a secret, isn't it?"

I sighed and hung my head. "Yeah, it is."

"I see. And y'all are...sleeping together?"

My head jerked up. "No," I said quickly. Then, I winced, realizing I'd sounded defensive again. "God, I do sound terrible, don't I?"

Eve laughed. "It's cute. Honestly. You sound like someone who has never had to lie a day in her life."

I flushed. "I never have."

"Must be nice," Eve muttered under her breath. "You look like you're going to combust. What's really going on with you two?"

And I *did* feel like I was going to burst. I had no one to talk to about this. I was way out of my depth. My brothers definitely could not know. Which meant Blaire and Piper were off-limits. And their friends, too, because I didn't trust any of them to keep a secret. But I no longer had a best friend, and it wasn't like I could tell my *dad*. What a disaster that would be.

Eve was here. She knew how to keep a secret. In fact, she'd come here to talk to me. For...some reason.

"You first," I said carefully. Even though I wanted nothing more than to blather on about my own angst. Maybe she'd be more willing to keep my secret if I knew one of hers.

"Ah," Eve said with a sigh. "Fair enough. I was actually here to ask about Whitton."

"Whitt?" I asked in surprise.

Eve smiled, and it wasn't her sharp smile that I'd seen her turn on guys. It was almost shy. "He's hot. We met at Campbell's birthday party. But he's new, and he doesn't run in any of my circles. The only person I know who knows him is...you."

"You want *me* to hook you up with Whitt?"

She laughed. "Oh no. I think I can do most of it on my own. I was just hoping for insider trading info, if you know what I mean." She winked at me.

"Uh, honestly, I only know what West has told me."

"No place where I could accidentally run into him again?"

"He's coming to Annie and Jordan's wedding. I bet you could talk to him there."

She wrinkled her nose. "So many people."

"I mean, I'm sure he'd be into you. What guy wouldn't be into you?"

Eve laughed hoarsely. "You're sweet. But plenty."

I had doubts. If I were a little more inclined to women, I totally would date her. She was gorgeous.

"Well, that'll have to be good enough. Thank you. Now, spill. You and Weston?"

"Okay, but don't tell anyone, please. My brothers can*not* find out."

"My lips are sealed."

I took a deep breath and then released it slowly before divulging the whole messy thing. From our early flirtation, him coming home from LA, the coaching session, to him fingering me in the living room. My face heated as I admitted all of it.

Eve's eyes were wide. "I'm sorry. He got you off that easily, and you didn't *bang* him?"

I laughed. "Uh, no. No, I did not."

"He didn't even try to push you into sex? Not even a blow job?"

"No, he proved his point and went to take a shower, as if he was utterly unaffected."

Eve straightened. "A shower, you say?"

"Yeah."

"Oh, sweet summer child," she said with a laugh. "Boy had to get away from you or else he was going to combust. That's the only reason he took that shower. I refuse to believe any other explanation. No one is that righteous."

"You think?"

She nodded emphatically. "Take it from someone

who knows. He wants you, and all you have to do is let him know that you want him, too."

"What if he doesn't?" I asked in a small voice.

"Wipe that from your mind. There's no room for doubt. And anyway, it's not like you have to marry the guy."

"That's true." I laughed.

She was right. For all I knew, West was going to be in LA for a lot longer than the next week or so. His job was in LA, just like Campbell's was. How much more time was I going to have with him?

"Plus, he *gave you* the playbook."

I blinked at her. "What do you mean?"

"He taught you all the things that guys like, right? He showed you how to flirt and what to talk about and how to carry on a conversation. He picked out your outfits and your drinks and made you come. He taught you seduction tactics, and the only way he knows them is because they work on him. It's what he likes."

"But it was just...universal information."

"No, it was from one guy about what he knows works. He knows this because from his experience, it has worked on *him*."

I rocked back in my chair. I'd never thought about it that way. He'd been teaching me how to get a guy, but specifically, it was how to get *him*. "Which means...I can use those tactics on *him*."

Eve grinned, and it was the sharp smile that meant she'd won. "Exactly. No guy is going to say no to a girl coming on to him. You can make him *crawl* for you."

14

WESTON

"It'll only be a week," Campbell said for the tenth time since we'd gotten on the plane back to LA.

"You don't have to convince me. Convince your wife."

Blaire had been less than pleased that we were already going back to LA after only being in Lubbock for such a short period of time. We were supposed to have a few months off. The band would be gone for a promotional tour and then an actual international tour for the new album. I didn't quite know where I fit in for all of it, but I'd recorded the whole damn thing, so I wasn't backing out now.

"It's one more song," Campbell grumbled.

We were headed straight to the studio to practice the new song with the rest of the band. I'd had to tell Nora this morning that I was heading out. She had known all along that I was going back to LA, but even I hadn't expected it to be this soon. It had only been a couple days since I'd gotten her off in the living room. I should have said something about it. But fuck, what could I have said?

I shouldn't have done it. I didn't fucking regret it. But if I was going to survive having her as my roommate, then I absolutely could not talk about it. Because talking about it would make it happen again.

I didn't trust myself enough for it not to happen.

And if I didn't want to end up with her bent over the kitchen counter with my cock buried inside of her, I needed to stay away. The real problem was that I *did* want that. I really wanted that.

When Campbell had mentioned flying into LA immediately to get this song out of his head, I'd practically jumped at the chance. Maybe some distance, however brief, would help.

Campbell sighed as he stared down at his phone. "I should have brought Blaire with me."

"Probably," I agreed.

"I mean...we've been trying..." He trailed off.

My eyebrows rose. "Fuck, man. Seriously?"

Campbell shot me a sheepish look. "Yeah. We want to get pregnant right away. I want a kid with her so bad, man. And well, she's fertile *this* week. Like, what are the fucking chances?"

I shrugged. I wanted kids. I knew that unprotected sex got you children. But I hadn't ever considered more than that. Definitely not fertility windows. "Why didn't you bring her?"

"She said she had *Blaire Blush* stuff planned."

Blaire was the owner of her own wellness blog. Over the holidays, she'd been on the *Today* show, talking about her advice column and wellness programs. She'd gone on a speaking tour for a few weeks after that, out there promoting her work. Her company had bloomed after her affiliation with Campbell, and we all loved to see how much success she had.

"Unfortunate. But fuck, I'm so happy for you, man. You're trying to have a kid. That's so adult of you."

Campbell snorted. "Yeah. Sometimes, I think, what the hell do I know about being a parent? My childhood was just two adults constantly yelling at each other."

"Yeah, but you're not your parents. You and Blaire love each other. You'll make great parents."

He smiled down at his phone. "Thanks, West."

I nodded at him. "It's the truth."

The car pulled up in front of the production studio headquarters, and we were ushered inside. Waiting for us outside of the studio was none other than the Cosmere manager, Bobby Rogers.

He held his arms out and smiled fondly at Campbell. "You're back! Good to see you, kid."

Campbell groaned. "Stop calling me kid, Bobby."

Bobby clapped him on the shoulder. "Always good to have the talent back in the building."

"We can hear you," Viv said. She appeared at his shoulder, rolling her big brown eyes. She brushed her bubblegum-pink hair out of her eyes and pulled Campbell into a hug and then me. "Hey, you."

"Good to see you," I told her. Viv was the bass player. Behind her was Santi, who played drums, and Yorke, on guitar.

"Just ignore him," Santi said boisterously. He hit Campbell's knuckles and then tipped his head at me. "We're glad you're home."

Home. LA wasn't home. I didn't know what was home anymore. Seattle had always been home, but now, only Mom was there. It was strange to think that Lubbock had become home in such a short period of time.

"Yo," Yorke said, as monosyllabic as Santi was animated.

"So, this new song," Bobby said. He arched an eyebrow at the pair of us.

"Shut it, Bobby," Campbell groaned. "Let me go play it for you."

"We listened to the demo," Santi said. "It needs a solid drumbeat."

"Obviously."

"But the keys are the spotlight," Bobby said, looking to me. "That your doing?"

I shrugged. "Campbell wanted keys. I delivered."

"Yeah. I wanted it to be keys heavy. I needed something that felt like it pulled you forward."

But I was still looking at Bobby. He'd been wary of me since I'd helped put the album together. As if at any moment, I was going to demand my fair share of the profits. The studio and I had worked out a payment schedule, as if I were recording as a backup. They wanted to cover their ass so that I didn't sue. Even though I had no intention of doing any of that. I'd get paid for what I deserved, but I wasn't a member of the band. And I didn't need their manager to glare at me to try to make me remember. I felt that every day of my life.

"Maybe we could talk to Michael to get him in on this one," Bobby suggested.

"No," Campbell barked at once. Michael was their old

keyboardist, but he'd ditched the band right before this album to spend more time with his family. "West will do it."

"Yeah, Bobby," Viv said with a wink. "We have West."

"I do miss Michael sometimes though," Santi said with a sigh.

"Before he turned into a wet blanket," Yorke said.

Everyone burst into laughter at that and agreed. The tension dissolved as only Yorke could pull off.

We were all rushed into the studio. I sat down at the keys. My mind was blissfully blank as the notes rushed up at me. Campbell's smooth voice took up the first verse. Then, it was a frenzy as I blew through the intricate melody I'd come up with. It was a sweeping song, and while maybe not my favorite on the new album, it was the best keys track.

We spent the next couple hours working on everyone else's pieces. It was grueling work but also my favorite part of the process. It was when the song went from an idea to reality.

We stumbled out of the studio late and drifted into the nearest nightclub. We'd been regulars here the last six months. I'd been schooled on all the things that I'd taught Nora Abbey about flirting and dating. I had no interest in any of that tonight.

"Fuck, that was satisfying," Santi said once we were escorted to a VIP booth.

"Definitely," Viv agreed.

Viv's girlfriend, Kris, nodded. "I'm glad that I got to hear it. I can't believe you put it together like that in a few hours."

"Oh, it's still shit," Campbell said. "We have hours more to hammer it out."

Kris huffed. "You could release exactly what you have now, and it'd be a hit."

"Yeah, but not up to his high standards, love." Viv kissed her on the cheek. "We've learned to let him be a perfectionist. It is what it is."

"But your part is *killer*," Santi cheered, slapping me on the chest. "Jealous."

I laughed. "Uh, thanks."

"Speaking of...who are you taking home tonight?"

He scanned the bar, but I shook my head.

"Nah. I'm good. I'm exhausted."

Campbell laughed. "From what? A few hours in the studio?"

"We flew here today," I said in my defense. When the real reason was that I wasn't interested in some easy ass. Not when the girl I couldn't stop thinking about was waiting two rooms over at home.

"Got a sweetheart back in Lubbock?" Santi teased.

"And how would I have done that in two weeks?"

"You move fast, *hombre!*"

"The only person he's seen since he's been in Lubbock is my little sister," Campbell said.

Santi crowed, "Ooh, you into his *sister*?"

"Whoa, whoa, whoa. I didn't say that," I said quickly.

"You're not an idiot," Viv said.

Yorke just nodded. "Suicidal."

"That's fucking right," Campbell said with a sharp grin. "Nora has been through enough."

"Nora's hot though," Santi said.

Campbell glared at him. "Take her name out of your mouth."

"Can't protect her forever," Viv said just to needle him.

"Look, her boyfriend cheated on her with her best friend, and she *found* them," Campbell said. "She was totally fucked up about it. She needs more time to get over it. Not any one of you shitheads interfering."

Santi held his hands up. "I'm just fucking with you, bro."

I said nothing. I wished that I could sink into the seat and disappear entirely.

"How's she doing anyway?" Campbell said. "She seemed fine at my birthday, but she hides it well."

I cleared my throat. "Uh, better. We've been going out to the bars sometimes to blow off steam."

Campbell narrowed his eyes. "Just you two?"

"Yeah, as *friends*," I said hastily. "I'm her roommate. So, it's easier. We just drive together."

"Wait, wait, wait," Santi said, leaning forward. "You *live* with his baby sister?"

"Yeah," I said softly.

Santi turned to Campbell. "And you allow this fucker to live with her?"

"You're talking about her like she's an object," Viv snarled. "She's a woman. She can do what or who she pleases. Fuck all of you misogynistic men!"

"She's right, Campbell," Santi said, preening. "Let her fuck whoever she wants."

"That's my little sister, you asshole."

"You're so controlling," Viv teased, poking his shirt.

"I'm not controlling. I don't want her to get hurt." He considered it for a second, and then his gaze shifted to me. "And I'd kill anyone who touched her."

"Not controlling," Viv said with a snort. "Yeah, right."

I met Campbell's gaze levelly, trying not to let him know I was sweating through my shirt. Fuck, fuck, fuck.

When he said *touch her*...did he mean the inside or outside of her?

He was going to kill me.

Literally kill me.

I'd already broken bro code. And there was no going back from what I'd done. But I could keep it together. I could make sure it never happened again.

15

NORA

A nnie paced back and forth across the bridal suite.

"Would you sit your ass down?" Sutton said with an eye roll. "I've gotten married this twice, and I was never this nervous."

"I'm not nervous," Annie said. "I passed my boards. *That* made me nervous."

Jennifer arched an eyebrow. "Then explain the pacing."

"It's taking too long," she said.

"You chose a five o'clock wedding," Sutton reminded her.

"I know. I know. Why didn't we get married at one? Better yet, why didn't we elope?"

"Because you'd have regretted it," I told her. "You know you want that big Wright wedding."

Annie smiled softly. She was a vision in a cream lace gown with an impressive V down the front, which tapered down to hug her hips appreciatively. Her red hair had been designed into an elaborate updo with loose tendrils falling purposely. "I do want that. I should have done a first look."

"David and I did. Took so much of the edge off." Sutton's smile dipped softly as she said, "But it was my second wedding."

"I think I'd want one," Jennifer said. "Less time to stress, and we all know that I have too much anxiety. I'd be a bigger mess than you."

Annie huffed. "I'm not a mess."

I laughed softly. She was a bit of a mess, but it was okay. I'd seen brides be way less sure than her about what they were about to walk into. Annie and Jordan had been made for each other. I was glad to be a part of their big day.

"Nora," my assistant, Tessi, called from the door.

"Have a drink," I told Annie. "It'll help. I'll be back when it's time."

Annie smiled brilliantly at me. "Thanks, Nora. You're the best!"

I waved her off and then headed out of the bridal suite.

"What's up?" I asked Tessi.

"You sure you don't want to be a guest at this wedding? I can handle it."

"I know you can. But this is my favorite part."

I'd brought Tessi on for the event to run the reception since I wanted to attend my friend's wedding. Jennifer had done much the same. She was the official Wright Vineyard photographer, and she'd brought her camera because she loved it, but since she was a bridesmaid, she'd gotten Annie to hire her friend for the wedding instead.

And I probably should have handed the whole thing off to Tessi, but I *loved* helping brides walk down the aisle. There was something so special about it.

"All right. No problem. Looks like almost everyone is here. I got the guys into place. Want to check it all over?"

I nodded and followed her to the barn door. The ceremony would be starting any minute. People were already flooding into seats on the Wright Vineyard lawn. We were lucky that the weather was picture-perfect. The first touch of spring with a clear blue sky and an abundance of sunshine.

My gaze skated across the crowd. It was the second-biggest event we'd had here. Only rivaled by Morgan Wright's wedding. As she was the CEO of Wright Construction, the family company, it had been unsurprising. But Jordan and Annie had nearly as big of a crowd.

But I was looking for one person in particular. And when my eyes found Weston Wright talking to his brother, it was like a pulse thrummed between us. He found my gaze and smiled.

"He's *cute*," Tessi said.

"He is."

"Yours?"

I bit my lip. "My roommate."

Tessi winked at me. "You have time. Go talk to him."

She pushed me out of the barn, and I nearly tripped forward on my high heels.

I laughed and shot Tessi a look. She just shrugged and gave me a thumbs-up.

"Hey," I said with a smile as I approached West and Whitt.

West had only gotten back last night. He'd waved at me when he got in and promptly passed out. I'd been too busy with wedding stuff all morning that I hadn't seen or talked to him. Which meant I hadn't been able to implement any of my new flirting techniques on him. I'd been pumped about it when Eve and I came up with the idea, but now, I was worried it was stupid.

But that smile on his face as I walked up to him sure helped matters.

"Hey, what a wedding," West said.

Whitton nodded. "You've done an incredible job here."

"Thank you."

Whitt gestured away. "I'm going to grab Harley and sit down. We'll save you a seat."

West waved him off. "Is Annie ready for this?"

"She's a little nervous, but yeah, I think she's more than ready."

"Good."

I reached up and took his tie in my hands. "Your tie is crooked."

West glanced down at himself. "I don't wear them often."

"I remember," I told him, looking up at him under my thick lashes.

The memory of him forgoing a tie in a button-up when we'd gone out came with the added reminder of his finger strumming my clit. The way he'd gotten me off that night. My cheeks flushed slightly as that hit me all at once.

Then, I pushed down the embarrassment and went back to fixing his tie. "There. That's better."

"Thanks," he said, clearing his throat.

"Of course." I forced myself to smile and get the words out. "I missed you."

"Yeah?" he asked softly.

"I know your life is crazy right now, but it's good to have you back in Lubbock. I'm sure you're going to be gone again soon."

He shrugged. "Maybe."

I'd always known West was going back to LA. It was something I'd purposely not thought of.

"Maybe?"

"I mean, I don't know. LA was different this time. But yeah, it's part of the job."

"What happened that has you so uncertain?"

"Just a feeling I got. Let's talk about it later."

"Okay. Well, I'm glad you're home. The house is empty without you."

Which was true, but oh the implications.

His eyes widened slightly, and then he looked away. Off toward where Campbell and Hollin were seated with Blaire and Piper. Then back to me. He looked conflicted. "Well, at least someone missed me here."

The music changed to announce the start of the wedding.

"I'm going to take a seat. I'll see you later, Snickers."

My pulse quickened. Fuck, I wanted him. I wanted *this*.

"Nora," Tessi said.

It was time.

Weston Wright would have to wait until after.

I hurried back to Tessi and into the bridal suite. "Showtime."

Annie grinned from ear to ear. "Let's do this."

I arranged everyone into position. Both girls were in matching navy-blue dresses with bouquets of white roses, festooned with eucalyptus leaves. Annie's father waited for her at his designated spot.

Tears came to his eyes when he saw his baby girl, and he pressed a kiss to her cheek. "You look beautiful, darling."

"Thanks, Dad," she said, fighting back tears.

Then, Peyton appeared, holding Aly's hand. "Your flower girl is here."

Annie's seven-year-old niece, Aly, twirled in her white dress with a navy-blue sash around her waist and a basket of rose petals in her hand. "I'm here, Aunt Annie."

"Oh, you look gorgeous, Aly."

Aly did another perfectly executed twirl, like the little ballerina she was. "Thank you. Miss Peyton helped do my hair."

"I love it," Annie said, admiring the twin braids that snaked into a crown atop her head.

Peyton squeezed Annie tight. "I love you. So glad to be your sister on this day."

"My sister always," Annie said.

Once Peyton got into her seat at the front, I took Aly's hand and gestured for her to do her thing. To her credit, she was spectacular. A performer through and through.

She didn't just toss her petals. She skipped and twirled and did little leaps, raining petals all over the aisle. Everyone appropriately oohed and aahed over her before she dropped into the seat next to Peyton and waved at her daddy. Isaac waved back from his spot as a groomsman, next to Julian.

I sent the bridesmaids down the aisle, and then it was Annie's turn. "Whenever you're ready."

The audience rose as Canon in D came on. Annie looked to her dad and nodded. She straightened her spine and then walked down the rose-strewn aisle. I stood with Tessi at the back in awe. We gripped each other's hand and sighed over the beauty of it all. My favorite part. The very best part.

Jordan got the first look of his bride. His jaw fell open at the sight of Annie walking down the aisle toward him. It was a one-of-a-kind look. A perfect, heart-wrenching moment that would be encapsulated in pictures and videos for all time. But right now, that look was just for her.

The rest of the wedding was as stunning as I'd thought it'd be. They had written their own vows, and most of the party was sniffling into tissues by the end of it, Tessi and me included.

But it was the first look by the groom that always did me in. The moment that I knew true love existed and no one could take it away. It was the moment I'd wanted for myself all those years. The one I'd fought for with August for nothing.

True love couldn't be destroyed.

It couldn't be buried.

It was effervescent and irrevocable and forever.

Maybe it made me a sap to believe in something that I'd seen fall apart firsthand with my parents. But pain didn't make love any less beautiful; it made it essential. And no one could ever convince me otherwise.

16

WESTON

Here I was, determined to stay away from Nora, and she had come over to tell me she...missed me. All I could think the whole time Annie and Jordan said their *I do*s was that Nora had missed me. That the house had been *empty* without me.

I'd barely been able to pull myself away. I wanted to dig into that comment. Was she saying what I thought she was saying? Because despite how I'd told myself I'd stay far away, I kept thinking about *her*, too.

Whitt stood at my side in the reception as we waited for the bride and groom to show up. Harley was on her phone, ignoring us both.

"Hey, did you miss Dad's call?" Whitt asked.

I shot him a look. "I saw that he called."

"He keeps asking about you."

"And why are you even answering his calls?"

Whitt shrugged. "Because he's still our dad."

I wrinkled my nose. "Debatable."

"His semen created half our DNA," Harley interjected. "But yeah, fuck him."

This was one of the few things that Harley and I agreed on. Whitt still talked to Dad. As if there were some reason to still talk to the man who had hidden us as a secret family while he was married to someone else. He was the one who had fucked up. I didn't owe him a damn thing.

Whitt sighed, as if he knew that he'd lost this battle again. "Fine. He just wants to congratulate you."

"He never wanted me to pursue music full time. Why would he congratulate me?"

"He was wrong."

Damn right he was.

"I'll believe it when he says that to my face."

"And how can he do that if you never talk to him?"

I rolled my eyes. I didn't care if Owen Wright ever congratulated me. I wasn't sure I'd believe it even then.

Whitt hit me. "Bro."

I glared at him to tell him I was done with this conversation. But his eyes were elsewhere.

"What?"

He pointed across the barn. I followed his finger past dozens of guests in their finest, sipping on drinks and eating finger food while they waited for the bride and groom to make their appearance, to the golden girl who had just stepped inside.

My heart stuttered. "Fuck," I whispered.

Whitt patted me twice on the back. "Good luck with that."

"What?" Harley asked. She looked between us all. "What are you talking about?"

Nora Abbey glided into the barn. She'd changed out of the floral dress she'd worn to work the ceremony and into a floor-length gold dress that made her look like a goddess. The dress plummeted between her breasts and left her arms bare, but the material swished delicately around her legs as she maneuvered the room, saying hello to everyone who knew her. She might be shy around guys, but she was in her element here.

"Oh," Harley whispered. "Is that Nora?"

"Yeah," I said, entranced.

"Well, she's a bit out of your league, isn't she?"

Whitt nudged Harley. "Seriously?"

"Look at her," Harley said with a laugh. "She's gorgeous."

"She is," I admitted out loud.

I was glad that Campbell and Hollin were on the other side of the room. That they hadn't seen that I was eye-fucking their sister from a distance.

A few minutes later, after she made her rounds, she walked toward me with Eve on her arm. Eve wore an emerald dress that matched her eyes, and her black hair was down in waves. But I barely noticed her. I couldn't say the same for my brother, who gripped the table tighter as she approached.

"Hey, handsome," Eve said, looking at Whitt.

"Eve," he said with a charming smile.

"You look..." I said, gesturing to Nora.

She ran her hands down the sides of her dress, accentuating her hips. "You think?"

"Stunning."

Harley huffed at all the hormones flying. "I'm going to go get a drink."

"No, you are not!" Whitt said at the same time I said, "Harley!"

She laughed. "Can't stop me."

Then, she disappeared. I ground my teeth together, and Whitt looked like he was about to follow her.

"Let her go," Eve said. "This is a safe place. She won't get into any trouble."

"You don't know my sister," Whitt said.

I couldn't disagree. "Harley finds trouble wherever it is."

Eve laughed. "I know all about that."

"Tessi will keep an eye on her," Nora said. "I gave her a list of minors ahead of time. There are a few of them."

Whitt still looked like he wanted to go off after her, but Eve was still standing there, admiring him up and down.

She touched the sleeve of his suit. "Mind if I steal you for a minute?"

Whitt's eyes shot back to Eve. The gentle touch, the familiar flirting. He nodded. "After you."

Eve shot him a simpering smile. She winked at Nora and then headed off with my brother, leaving us all alone.

"Well, they're unexpected," I admitted.

Nora shrugged. "Eve is the kind of girl who goes after what she wants." Her eyes flicked up to mine. A small, knowing smile came to her lips.

I should resist that smile. The look from under her

lashes. The way she leaned in toward me. Yep, I should definitely walk away from this.

"The wedding turned out amazing."

"Thank you," she said brightly. "I was pleased."

"You have a talent."

Her eyes moved around the room and then back to me. "I was told not to talk about weddings right away, but hey, we're *at* a wedding, right?"

I blinked at her. "Nora...I...this..."

She laughed softly. "Oh man, am I that bad at this?"

"That bad at...what?"

"Flirting," she said, biting her lip.

"You're flirting with me?"

"I mean, apparently, I am not good at it."

"No," I said quickly. "You're not bad at it."

"Okay. I'll keep practicing then," she said with a wink.

I clenched my hands on the table to keep from reaching for her. She was playing me at my own game. And it was working.

"Did you practice while I was gone?"

Her eyes were guileless. "Why would I do that?"

"Because you said that you wanted to move on. You wanted to flirt and date and all that."

"I did. I do," she said firmly. "And I can't say that everything is perfect, but I have moved on. And I want to flirt and date and all that."

"But you didn't while I was out of town?"

"I didn't," she confirmed. "Did you...see anyone when you were out of town?"

I shook my head automatically. "We went out, but I wasn't interested."

She bit her lip, and it looked like she wanted to ask why. But of course, I couldn't explain *why*.

"LA was sort of a lot anyway."

She took the segue for what it was. She put another step of distance between us. "What happened in LA? You didn't mention that things were different when we were texting. Did something happen?"

"I don't know. It's probably nothing, but I got a bad feeling that the Cosmere manager doesn't like me."

"Bobby? What did he do to make you think that?"

"Nothing. He made some offhand comments about bringing Michael back, about letting another keyboardist record the new song. That sort of thing. Nothing concrete, but it makes me think he's going to try to get me cut."

"Can he do that?"

I shrugged. "Probably."

"But why would he even do that? You're Campbell's best friend."

"That's why. Bobby thinks he has less influence on him when I'm there. And look, I'm only trying to help. I didn't ask for anything that's been given. Everything that has happened has been at Campbell's insistence."

"Which Bobby hates?"

"Yes." I shrugged. "I'm sure he'd rather I take the production offer from the studio than to keep working directly with Cosmere."

Nora's lips pursed. "I'm sure he would. But you don't want that?"

"I'd be lying if I said I didn't want to keep working

with Cosmere. But that offer is better than anything I've ever had before."

"Last resort," she mused.

"It's a pretty good last resort. Just waiting to see where all of this goes, and Bobby Rogers didn't make me feel any better about it."

"Hmm...have you talked to my brother about this?"

"Nah, I don't want to bug him."

"But it sounds serious."

"It's not. Like I said, just a feeling." My eyes returned to hers. "Don't worry about it."

"If you say so." She looked skeptical, and honestly, I felt the same way. I didn't know how to broach it with Campbell anyway.

We were kept from saying anything else with a music change to announce Jordan and Annie Wright. They moved immediately into their first dance, and then the buffet opened.

"I'm going to check on something with Tessi. Save me a seat?" Nora said.

"Sure. I can do that."

"And a dance," she said with another smile before disappearing.

As I watched her skirt swish away, I knew that I was truly and utterly fucked. I'd been able to deflect for a moment, but I wasn't sure how long I could hold out. How long I wanted to hold out.

I glanced up and found Campbell's eyes on me. How long had he been watching? Did he know? I nodded my head at him, and he waved me over.

"Got you a seat."

"Thanks."

And I swore it wasn't strange to hold the seat next to me for his sister. She would be sitting here normally anyway...right?

———

I'd worried for nothing.

The rest of the reception went off without a hitch. Nora and I danced in the crowd of people to all the typical wedding songs. I only got a look from Campbell once when Nora and I slow danced and she rested her cheek against my chest. I held her tight to me and pretended that I couldn't see his glare. Blaire hit him to get him to leave us alone.

Nora laughed with a flush on her face at the whole thing. At one point, Whitt and Eve slipped out.

"Did you see that?" Nora said, gesturing to the door.

My phone dinged in my pocket, and I checked the message from Whitt.

See you later.

I waggled my eyebrows at her. "Well, well..."

"Think he can handle Eve?" Nora asked with a wink.

"Oh, she might not even be crazy enough for him."

She gaped at me. "Eve? *Eve*?"

I laughed. "Oh, the stories I could tell."

"I would never have guessed. He seems so buttoned up."

"Oh, he is." I glanced around the room. "Mostly, I'm surprised he left without Harley."

Nora followed my line of sight and found my baby sister dancing with Chase Sinclair. I took a step forward as anger coursed through me. She grabbed my arm to stop me.

"Hey, leave her."

"She's nineteen," I growled.

"They're just dancing."

"One, I thought you hated the Sinclairs. And two, isn't he thirty?"

"I don't hate Chase, and I think he and Annie are the same age. Twenty-nine?" she said, watching them move together.

"That's a ten-year age gap."

"They're *just* dancing," she reminded me. "Just like us."

Our eyes met as we twirled under the chandelier light.

"Fine. I'll let them dance. But she is not leaving with him."

Nora laughed lightly. "I'm sure Chase would like the distraction, but even he's not dumb enough to take home a teenager."

"Why would he need the distraction?"

"Oh right. Sometimes, I forget you weren't here for all the drama. Annie and Chase were best friends growing up. Both always thought they'd end up together, but obviously...she just married Jordan."

"And he still showed for the wedding?"

"Yep."

"But he still loves her?"

"Yep."

"Damn," I said softly.

I glanced back over at him laughing with my little sister. That was *never ever* happening as far as I was concerned. I ignored how hypocritical that sounded, coming from me. But I couldn't deny he needed the distraction. Just so long as it didn't go past dancing.

"Leave them be," Nora said, pulling me back into the dance.

As the night wore on, I watched Chase and Harley dance a half-dozen more times.

When all was said and done, I stood with a sparkler in my hand as Annie and Jordan walked down the makeshift aisle to the old-timey car they'd rented for the occasion. They kissed at the apex as we cheered for them and then drove off into the night.

Harley was still talking to Chase as the crowd dissolved around them. I grabbed her arm as soon as Chase headed to the parking lot.

"Don't think about it."

"Think about *what*?" she snapped at me.

"He's, like, ten years older than you."

"So?" she said with a laugh. She shook me off. "I'm not stupid. I'm going home."

"Good. Be sure you do."

"Having older brothers is the worst," she said as she stomped off.

I sure hoped that she took my advice. She usually only listened to Whitt.

"Still worried about her?" Nora asked.

I nodded.

"She'll be fine. Come on. Help me and Tessi clean up."

I watched Harley disappear and then followed Nora back into the barn. By the time we were through, the place looked abandoned. No one would have guessed there had been a wedding inside.

"I'll do the rest in the morning," she said with a yawn. "What a night."

"A great night."

"It was." She smiled up at me and then slung her arm through mine, resting her head against my arm. Even in her heels, she wasn't tall enough to reach my shoulder.

I didn't object. There was no one to see us anyway. "Let's get you home."

I drove us back to my place. Nora kicked off her shoes in the entranceway and covered a yawn.

"I've been up since the sun," she said. "And somehow, I'm exhausted *and* wired."

"Must be part of the job."

She nodded. "It is." She turned back to me, a devious smile coming to her face. We'd been walking on a tightrope all night. We'd laughed off her flirting earlier, but now, here we were again...all alone. "I had a good night with you, West."

"Me too."

She took a step closer. We weren't touching, but we were fucking close enough that it would be obvious what was happening if anyone were around.

"Thanks for letting me practice on you all night."

My blood heated. I wanted to practice on her some more. How much longer could I hold this back?

"Nora," I said.

"I like when you say my name like that."

"Like what?"

She looked up at me. "Like you can't get enough of saying it."

"I can't," I said.

She was stunning in her golden gown with those perfectly pink lips and her beckoning blue eyes. She had been flirting with me all night. We'd been skating this line for much longer than that.

"But I'm going back to LA. You know I'm going back."

She smiled invitingly up at me. "I know, but I want this anyway."

And maybe I was a bad friend for considering this. But there was a fine line, and I'd already crossed it. I might as well make it worth it.

"Come here," I commanded.

Her eyes widened slightly, as if she hadn't thought that any of this would work.

I drew her into me, tipping her chin up to look at me. Her heart was hammering in her chest, and she trembled slightly under my touch.

"Do you want more practice?"

She shivered. "Yes."

"What do you want?"

She bit her lip and said nothing. It had all gotten very serious. And I couldn't walk back from that line. I was too far gone. I'd thought of nothing but her since I'd made her come on my fingers.

I wanted her. She wanted me. Fuck everything else.

"This?" I asked, dipping down until our lips nearly touched.

Her eyes fluttered closed, and she released a soft sigh.

"Tell me."

"Yes."

"Tell me again that you want this."

"I want this," she nearly pleaded.

And I was undone.

My lips fitted to hers. Our first kiss. Our first everything.

17

NORA

Even when I'd dreamed of flirting with Weston, I hadn't quite believed that it would work. And now, he was *kissing me*.

It might be practice, but it felt like so much more. It felt like worlds had collided, the universe was singing just for us, the entirety of existence had slowed to this moment.

I'd been kissed before.

I'd never been kissed like this.

Weston cupped my jaw with one hand as his other slipped around my waist and dragged me hard against him. I was so much shorter than him that he had to bend forward at the waist to get to my lips. Our kiss was soft at first but picking up momentum.

He walked me through the kitchen until my back hit the counter. He released me long enough to grip behind my thighs and hoist me up. My ass hit the cold countertop, and I yelped in surprise. He smiled against my lips as he shoved his way between my open legs.

"Oh!" I gasped.

The only material separating us was the flow of my gold dress and his suit pants. He pressed hard against me as he brought both hands to my jaw and stole another kiss. His tongue slid against the seam of my lips. I opened to him and he entered my mouth like an invader coming to conquer. His movements were swift, determined, and oh-so fucking tempting. I could never predict what he was going to do next. The way he took control.

I realized then that Weston Wright had been holding back. He'd been *really* holding every single thing back in every interaction. If *this* was who he really was, then I had no idea how he'd kept his cool for as long as he had. How he'd even gotten me off without taking more from me.

"Fuck," he groaned into my mouth. "Fucking fuck, Nora."

My breath came out in pants. "Yes."

"I need more. I need all of you."

I pulled back to look at him. To see the desirous look in his eyes. "I won't deny you a thing."

He smirked, a devilish thing. "Be careful what you wish for."

I stole another kiss. "This is what I want. You showed me exactly what I want."

"And what exactly do you want?" he asked. He brushed a stray curl away from my cheek.

"You."

"You sure you're ready for that?"

I knew what he was asking. I'd been with exactly one person. And that person had betrayed me in every way that mattered. But over the months, I'd learned to trust my body...my heart with Weston. Time and time again, it was him who had made me want to keep trying and him who had shown me how. I wanted him to show me more.

"Yes."

"We can stop at any time if you change your mind."

"I won't need to stop." I'd made up my mind.

"Then come here."

He leaned forward and nipped at my bottom lip, sucking it into his mouth. I moaned softly and squirmed against him. Which only made me gasp again as I felt the fullness of his dick with every movement. He was hard as a rock, and, just from my limited guessing...*big*.

My hands fisted into the material of his shirt, tugging him closer and closer. Until our chests were pressed together, my legs were wrapped around his waist, and his dick was practically sealed against me. Even the light friction was sending sparks flying through me. It had been a long ten months of going without. I'd come apart on his fingers. What would it be like with him inside of me?

"Oh God," I gasped as he moved to kiss down my exposed throat.

He released my jaw, slipping his hands over my shoulders to my waist before landing on my hips. He gripped tightly. My ass was nearly off the counter as we rocked back and forth, rubbing against one another through our clothing.

I wanted and needed more. So much more. I was on fire. My body felt like it could burst into flames at any moment.

"I need..." I trailed off, lost to the intense sensations.

"What do you need?"

He pressed me back until I was on my elbows on the countertop. It wasn't big enough to lay me out completely, but he could get a full look at me while our bottom halves were still held roughly joined together.

"You," I breathed.

His hands swept up to the low cut of my dress, dragging a finger down the middle of my cleavage. "This?"

I bit my lip. "Maybe a little lower."

He arched an eyebrow. "Eager?"

"Should I not be?" I asked, utterly wanton.

"I've been waiting for this. I plan to indulge in every inch of you."

I flushed all over at those words. "Oh, well then, be my guest."

He hooked a finger under the material of my dress and slid it over my nipple. My head fell backward at the rush of sensation. I made a noise of delight and then his finger disappeared.

My eyes cracked open. "What?"

But he tipped his hands under the straps of my dress. They fell off my shoulders, and I slipped my arms out of them. He popped the clasp on my strapless bra, letting my breasts spill forward from their enclosure.

His face was one of awe.

"Remember when you were trying on dresses for me?" he asked as he began to kiss his way down the front of my cleavage. His hands moving to cup my breasts.

"Ye-yes."

"That was torture."

"It was?"

"Pure torture," he said as he flicked his tongue against a nipple. "I owe *you* some torture for that."

"Oh," I said softly and then inhaled sharply as he dragged the entire nipple into his mouth.

He sucked it in and then bit teasingly on it, all while his fingers worked the other nipple to a peak. I practically lost consciousness as he flicked and bit and licked at my breasts. I'd had guys ogle them. I'd had them appreciate how full and perky they were. I had never had anyone worship them.

My legs gripped his hips so hard, begging for friction. I was soaking wet already. Was it possible to orgasm from him teasing my nipples?

"Please," I gasped.

His kisses stalled as he looked up at me with that grin on his face that said he knew exactly what he was doing. Then, he went back to caressing my breasts. He was not oblivious to my pants and demands. He was determined to torture me like this. Even though it sent a thrill through me to know he'd been this affected by my dresses.

Suddenly, his kisses moved south. I went rigid as his mouth went from my skin back down to the material of the dress. His hands bunched up the skirt of the dress so he could drag his hands up my inner thighs, stopping just short of where I was so desperate for him.

"Should I torture you some more?" he teased.

"West," I groaned.

A finger tracked down the middle of my lace underwear. I jumped at the contact.

He just grinned, shooting me that hidden dimple. "As I expected. You're so wet."

I blushed at the words, but his head had already disappeared beneath my skirts. And then his *mouth* was on my underwear, right over my opening. He didn't move the material out of the way; he just breathed hot air against it.

"Oh fuck."

He did it again and again. I writhed underneath him, desperate for release. How was I this close? *How*? It shouldn't have been possible. And yet my core was pulsing as everything built up and up and up.

When he hooked my thong and dragged it down my legs, I could barely contain myself.

"How close are you?" he asked as he slicked a finger through my folds, coating it with my wetness.

"Close."

He circled my clit.

"So close."

His mouth replaced his finger, sucking on my clit. My head hit the tiles of the kitchen wall with a soft crack.

"Oh *my* God," I gasped.

He followed the gentle licking with two fingers thrusting deep inside of me. And I saw stars. He didn't even have to move. He'd worked me up so much that the first few strums against my clit caused me to come undone.

I cried out in incoherent sputters. Time had disappeared as the orgasm racked my body. It was a minute later when everything finally stopped shuddering and the earthquake in my body settled.

West was watching me with delight on his face. "I barely touched you."

I laughed softly. "That's what you call barely touching me?"

He withdrew his fingers and helped me off the countertop and onto wobbly legs. My knees buckled underneath me. He caught me easily and swept me up into his arms. I tried to protest, but he was already heading down the hallway toward his room.

In all the months of him being away, I'd never touched West's room, except to keep it clean. Now, it felt as if I were entering the West Wing for the first time. He toed the door closed behind him and then set me down in the middle of his king-size bed. He flicked on a side lamp, which illuminated all the hard contours of his body as he stripped out of his suit coat and ripped free the buttons on his shirt.

I sat up onto my knees and ran my hand down each individual ridge. "Mmm." My hand moved to his belt, and I wrenched it free, popped the button, and dragged down his zipper. "This is much better."

"Is it now?" he asked with that same feral look in his eyes. As if he'd never believed we'd get to this moment and he was going to take advantage of every single minute of it.

"Oh yes."

"And that dress?"

I shimmied the rest of the way out of it, dropping it onto the floor. Now, I was completely naked in front of him. I wanted to wrap my arms across my breasts or sneak under the covers to hide from him. But he was entranced at the sight of me, and it stilled my arms as I lay backward on the bed for his viewing pleasure.

"Much better."

He dropped his trousers and kicked them off to the side. His cock sprang free of his boxers as he slipped them down his muscled legs. My eyes widened. I'd felt the hardness of him in the kitchen, but the sight of him was something else entirely.

"Oh," I whispered.

He crawled onto the bed after me, slipping his hips between my legs but just far enough away that he wasn't quite touching me yet. "Those are some wide eyes."

I reached out tentatively and wrapped my hand around his cock. It was his turn for his eyes to roll back into his head.

"You're big," I admitted softly.

"We'll go slow."

I dragged my hand up and down him a few times before he moved forward and captured my lips again. At the first contact of him against my core, I gasped into his mouth. He wasn't even in me, just slicking himself through my folds, and every single nerve ending crackled with desire.

"Nora," he breathed.

"Yes."

"Are you sure?" he repeated, pulling back to look into my face.

"I don't want to stop."

He nodded, reaching across the bed to grab a condom out of a side table. He broke the foil and sheathed himself. Our bodies aligned perfectly. His hand returned to my cheek as he tipped me up for a kiss.

When he pulled back, he searched my eyes for a hint of regret or a wish to stop. But I had none of that. I wanted this. I'd made my mind up long before we got here.

"Please," I said, tilting my hips up to try to get him to move.

"I can deny you nothing."

Then as promised, he moved forward. So, so slow at first. Just the head. In and out. An inch at a time as he stretched my awaiting body. Until he was buried all the way inside of me. I was so full, as I'd never been before. Not quite painful because I was so warmed up, but it was almost uncomfortable.

Then he withdrew and all of that evaporated. Pleasure hit me as West retreated and crashed back into me. Sweat beaded on our joined bodies as he took everything I was giving him. As I offered myself up on a platter.

He sat up and gripped my hips, thrusting somehow deeper inside of me. My eyes were tightly closed as moans left my mouth, and I pushed my hands into my hair.

"Are you going to come again?" he asked in a breathless pant.

Miraculously, I was. I'd never come during sex. And I was starting to think that I had been grossly misinformed about a lot of shit. Because this was incredible. This was mind-blowing. This was everything I'd always wanted.

And then I stiffened all over, contracting tight around his cock as I came entirely unexpectedly.

I cried out into the bedroom, and then West joined my shouts with a roar of his own as he unleashed inside of me. He jerked forward twice as he spent himself and then dropped forward over me.

"Oh," I whispered. "Oh wow."

"Yeah. Fuck."

"That was..." I had no words. I just stared at the ceiling in shock.

West withdrew and got rid of the condom. "That was...amazing."

"Yes."

"Worth it," he said softly against my shoulder as he drew me into him. "Sweet dreams."

And I smiled at the words that I'd said to him after catching him coming out of the shower. Oh, how sweet my dreams had been then. Now, my dreams were a reality.

Suddenly, the entire day weighed down on me. All that exhaustion I'd been holding hung heavy over me. I was warm and spent with my roommate pressed naked against my back. I couldn't have stayed awake if I wanted to.

18

WESTON

When I yawned awake the next morning, Nora was still naked in my arms. The light was blinding through my windows. I cursed myself for not having gotten any kind of curtains up yet. I'd never been a morning person in my life, and I certainly wasn't one today.

I tried to move my arm, but she made a noise of protest and snuggled in closer. It was the most adorable thing that I'd ever seen in my life. I should have felt an ounce of regret for what had happened last night. But I didn't.

I'd tried to stay away from Nora. When she'd looked at me like that and told me she wanted me, how could anyone fucking blame me?

Well, I had a feeling that Campbell would blame me.

I cringed at that thought.

Right. Last night had been a dream, and reality was creeping in with the morning sunlight.

Campbell Abbey was not forgiving, and he had a

temper. I'd seen it firsthand. He hadn't forgiven Michael for quitting the band. They still hadn't reconciled over it. The rest of the band had spent time with Michael and worked out their differences. But as much as Campbell loved Michael—and I knew he did—he hadn't even let Michael help in production on the album.

Campbell might be my best friend, but I wasn't exempt from his anger. And the easiest way to rile it was disloyalty. However he saw that.

With a sigh, I rolled my arm out from under Nora. She tugged the covers tighter around her. The urge to crawl back under those covers and pleasure her until she cried out again was unmistakable. If I didn't get out of this room right now, I'd do just that.

So, I threw on a pair of boxers and headed into the kitchen. Maybe some coffee would clear my head.

I heard the buzzing once the pot was percolating. Locating my phone, which had somehow been discarded on the kitchen table, I realized I'd missed a few calls from Campbell.

I swallowed. "Fuck."

Then, I called him back. "Hey, man."

"Where the fuck have you been all morning? It's almost noon. I'm halfway to your place."

My eyes shot wide. "What? Why? What happened?"

"I'll tell you when I get there."

"Sure." I hoped that my voice sounded calm and not like I was freaking the fuck out.

"Be there in five." Campbell ended the call.

I launched across the room, ignoring the coffee entirely and rushing back to my bedroom.

"Fuck, fuck, fuck," I muttered.

Campbell hadn't sounded mad, which meant he didn't know what had happened last night. He wouldn't have bothered calling me if he'd found out about Nora. He would have shown up and put his fist through my face. But that didn't mean I wanted him to show up now and do it.

I scrambled into the room. "Nora."

She groaned and rolled back over. "Sleep," she muttered in the softest voice, which made me want to crawl right back in there with her.

"Campbell's on his way."

Her eyes flew open. "What?"

"Campbell is on his way here right now. He called and said he was five minutes out."

She wrenched upward, tugging the sheet tight to her breasts. "Fuck."

"Pretty much."

She ran a hand back through her hair. Her eyes slid down my exposed chest and down lower, lower, lower to my boxers. "That's disappointing. I was having a really good dream."

My cock twitched at the implication in those words. "What sort of dream?"

Her cheeks showed a hint of pink. "If only we had time..."

I looked to the ceiling, cursing Campbell's name. "If only."

Nora looked suddenly self-conscious as she searched the floor for her dress. We'd kicked it to the other side of the room at some point. I went and grabbed it, handing it to her.

She blushed again, and I hastily turned around, so she could tug it back over her head. I felt ridiculous since I had literally kissed every inch of her yesterday. But this wasn't how I'd planned to wake her up either.

A loud knock came from the door.

"Fuck," I spat.

When I turned back around, Nora blanched. "I'll change and come out in a minute."

I nodded, and then she was gone, dashing down the hall to her room. The door creaked closed as I threw on a pair of shorts and snagged a T-shirt. I was pulling it over my head when I reached the front door.

"Hey, man," I said when I found Campbell in the doorway.

"Hey," he said, barreling inside. "Where's Nora?"

I shrugged. Did I look nonchalant? "Still sleeping."

Campbell wrinkled his nose. "I thought she still had cleanup at the winery this morning."

Shit. I'd forgotten. Neither of us had set an alarm. Hadn't exactly been on our brains.

"Maybe she left then. I just got up."

I headed to the coffee machine and poured myself a cup to have something to do with my hands.

"You're never going to believe the call I got this morning," Campbell said.

"What's that?"

"We're playing *The Tonight Show*."

Well, he was right about that. I never would have fucking guessed. "You're shitting me."

Just then, a door opened, and a fully dressed Nora stepped out. She yawned. "What's going on?"

"We're playing *The Tonight Show*," I told her.

"Really? That's great!"

"Why aren't you at the winery for cleanup?" Campbell asked.

Nora's eyes widened slightly. She was not good at hiding her thoughts, but thank fuck she didn't look over at me. "I didn't realize how late it was. Yesterday must have wiped me out. I bet Tessi is wondering where I am."

"Can we get back to the matter at hand? We're playing *The Tonight Show*?"

"Yeah. I heard from Bobby. He said they're going to drop the first single this week, and we'll play in New York City the following Friday."

My eyes widened. "A single already? I didn't think we were even planning an album drop for a few months."

"Still the plan, but we're going to start building suspense for it. With all of Blaire's footage, people already know it's coming. It's a matter of when."

It was my first real album release. I'd played with a ton of no-name bands, but this was a whole new level. I had no experience here. I was just going with the flow.

"What are we releasing?"

"We're going to drop 'Rooftop Nights.'"

I nodded. We'd talked about which songs to release when we were recording in LA. "Rooftop Nights" was the strongest song with a wicked beat and a fun chorus. I always thought it was going to be the party song of the summer.

"That sounds incredible," Nora said.

"We're leaving a week from Wednesday. Bobby is going to send a private plane for us with the rest of the band."

"And he wants me to play keys?"

Campbell shot me a strange look. "Of course you're playing keys."

"And Bobby is okay with that?"

"Bobby isn't the fucking band. I don't give a shit what he wants. You're playing the keys at the show." Campbell then paused before continuing, "Unless you don't want to."

"Fuck yeah, I want to."

"Awesome."

We clapped hands. It was all getting so fucking real. I wasn't an official member of the band by any stretch, but I was going to play *The Tonight Show*. This was a once-in-a-lifetime experience. I wasn't going to squander it. Plus, it might put some much-needed distance between me and Nora.

"What about you, shrimp?" Campbell asked. "Do you have a wedding that weekend?"

"I don't. Pretty much every weekend after that though."

Campbell grinned. "Then pack your bag. I'm taking you to New York."

Or maybe not.

Maybe there would be even less distance.

We carefully avoided eyes until Campbell finished his spiel and headed out. Finally, Nora looked up at me.

"Well, that's amazing for you. Playing *The Tonight*

Show with Cosmere. That's what you've always wanted, isn't it?"

I couldn't deny it.

"It is."

She bit her lip. She looked so uncertain in that moment.

"Are we still cool?" I asked her.

"Oh yeah, of course," she said quickly. Quicker than I would have liked. "Last night was fun."

"It was more than fun." I stepped up to her and drew her chin up to look at me. "It was incredible."

"But Campbell still can't know, right?" she said with a laugh. "I mean, I don't want you to get your face punched in for no reason."

"It's probably best if he doesn't know what happened."

She opened her mouth, as if she wanted to say more, and then closed it.

"Tell me what you're thinking, Nor."

"Does that mean...it can't happen again?"

And God fucking help me, I wanted to carry her right back into my room and fuck her all over again.

"Do you *want* it to happen again?"

She didn't move for a moment, and then she slowly nodded. "Don't you?"

"Yes, but I don't want to hurt you. I'm still planning to go back to LA. My job is volatile. I don't know what I can give you."

"I know you're leaving," she said, running her fingers up my chest. "I know you can't give me anything. But I want it anyway."

I could feel it in every fiber of my being that she was going to be the death of me. But I wanted every ounce of her, even knowing it had to end.

So, I hoisted her beautiful body into my arms and carried her back to my bed, where she belonged. We didn't resurface for a good long while.

PART IV

SECRETS, SECRETS

19

_____

WESTON

"You ready for this?" Campbell asked at my side.

"Ready as I'll ever be."

He clapped a hand on my back. "It's just another show."

I nodded as he wandered back to his wife. Blaire snuggled into his side as we waited for our chance to get onto _The Tonight Show_ stage. Nerves bit into me. It was just another show. And that might have been true for the rest of the band. They'd played _The Tonight Show_. They'd played hella bigger shows than this.

But me? No way. No fucking way.

I'd never played anything like this. And I felt grossly out of my league.

Even though we'd had a rehearsal on the stage earlier that morning. Everything had felt surreal then, but it had been easier. No expectations. Just playing "Rooftop Nights," like I had with the band a hundred times before this. Now, the host was onstage, the audience was waiting, and the performance would be broadcast to millions.

"Hey," Nora said, coming to my side.

Nora at my side made sense. Made all the voices of inadequacy quiet. They might come later, but right now, she was here.

"Hey."

"You excited?"

"Uh," I said, looking back to the stage.

She looked around once and then touched my arm. "Hey, back to me."

I jerked back to her face. Drowned in those big blue eyes. Let her ground me in the ocean of her eyes. "I might be out of my depth."

She laughed softly. "No, you're not. You're going to be incredible. You don't know how to be anything else."

"I've never done anything like this. My first performance with Cosmere, and it's *this*?"

"Yeah, and everyone will see what I see in you. That you're talented and you deserve your spot."

"And here I thought, we were talking about something else."

She smacked my arm. "Let's hope the rest of the world isn't sleeping with you."

I grinned down at her. "Only you have that privilege."

She snorted. "Privilege," she said with mock derision. "Men. Always so sure of themselves."

"I don't hear you complaining when you're moaning my name into the night."

"Give me credit," she said. I arched an eyebrow at her. "I moan your name during the morning and afternoon, too."

I chortled and realized what she'd done—she'd set

me at ease. Now, I was thinking about having her morning, afternoon, and evening, as I had for the last two weeks. No one was any the wiser about what was happening with us, but fuck, it was amazing.

I still worried sometimes that I wasn't giving her everything she deserved. But I couldn't offer more. I didn't know when I'd be yanked back to LA, and it didn't seem fair to her to begin a relationship when it could be stolen at any moment. We weren't Blaire and Campbell. This wouldn't end in a happily ever after. No matter how over-the-moon happy I was to be with her.

"You're a good distraction."

She grinned. "Then I did my job."

An assistant appeared in the doorway and announced the fifteen-minute warning.

"I should get ready."

"Good luck!"

She'd headed back to the girls when my phone buzzed in my pocket. I should turn the damn thing off. Just what I needed was random vibrations in my pocket while I was onstage. *Super professional, West.*

I went to switch it off and saw *Dad* appear on the screen. I ground my teeth together. Whitt's words were in my ear, saying that Dad wanted to congratulate me. That I should give him a chance. But damn, how many chances did he deserve? He'd messed up so many times that I wasn't sure I could count that high. Time and time again, all he had done was screw everything up.

And yet, when I saw him calling fifteen minutes before I went onstage for the biggest show of my life, all I could think about was Dad giving me my first guitar.

Mom had gotten me into keys at only five. I took to it like a swimmer to water. But Dad got me a guitar and paid for the lessons when he saw how fast I'd picked it up on my own. He paid for *all* the lessons. Whenever a new instrument interested me, he didn't ask, *What about the guitar I got you?* or, *Are you still playing the saxophone?* He'd handed over the money and listened to me play when he was in town.

We had a fraught, complicated relationship. Despite giving me the instruments, I knew that he didn't think music was a real career. Plus, he had spent more time with his "real" family in Vancouver than our fledgling family he'd hidden in Seattle. Jordan and Julian got the best of him while the rest of us got the scraps. But I'd clung to those scraps for so long that it was hard to completely ignore that call when I was already nervous and wanted to hear my dad's words of wisdom.

"Hello?" I said when I answered the phone.

"West," my dad said with relief in his voice.

"Hey, I don't have a lot of time. I'm about to go on."

"I know. Whitt told me about the performance. I'm so proud of you."

I choked on my words. "Thanks."

"I have the TV on already. I'm going to watch."

And it was so difficult to keep it together. Because all I'd ever wanted was my father's approval until I realized too late that none of it fucking mattered. He wasn't the person I'd thought he was. He'd never be the person I most looked up to in the world. He'd wrecked it all.

Still, that warred with everything I'd wanted for so

many years. A conflicting melee in my brain that was probably the last thing I needed before I went onstage.

"Okay...I have to go."

"Call me some other time. I just want to talk."

He never *just* wanted to talk.

"Maybe," I said uncertainly.

"I'm not the monster you've made me out to be."

"I thought you were a god," I ground out. "You made yourself into a monster."

And then I remembered all too well why I shouldn't have fucking answered. There was always an angle. Always a saint complex.

"West," he said softly.

But I hung up. I didn't need any more of that in my brain.

Campbell was beckoning me over when I got off the phone. "Ten minutes. You set?"

I must have still been vibrating with anger. Anger at my dad and myself. I should have known better. I *had* known better, and I had done it anyway.

I clenched my hands into fists and nodded. "Sure."

Campbell looked unconvinced, but we didn't have time. "All right. Let's get into position. We'll be announced, and then let's kill it."

Santi shrugged his shoulders back and bounced from foot to foot. "I'm fucking ready."

Viv popped a bubble in her gum. "Hell yeah."

Yorke grunted. Typical.

"Remember, 'Rooftop Nights' is already the number one song in the world," he said with a wicked grin. "We just have to prove to them why."

That thought only spiked my anxiety. I still couldn't believe that a song that I'd worked on was number one in the *world*. It was normal for Cosmere to have that sort of success, but this was the first song I'd ever worked on that had done anything. And now, I had to prove why I was out there, playing keys for the band instead of Michael. No pressure.

Campbell hit my shoulder again. "Wright, it's going to be fun."

I released my fists, trying to force in some calm. "Fun, right."

Santi laughed. "It's his first big show, Campbell Soup. Give him a break. You practically pissed yourself at our first big show."

"I did not," Campbell growled.

Viv blew another bubble. "Close enough."

Yorke tipped his head at me. "You'll be fine."

And from Yorke, that was real encouragement.

"Yeah, we wouldn't have you out there with us if you weren't the shit, *hombre*," Santi said.

"What he said," Campbell said.

We got a thumbs-up from the assistant, and I followed them onto the stage. I sat down in front of the keyboard. Bright lights hit me, and a bead of sweat dripped down my spine. Everything was blurry, as if I had no idea where the keys were anymore. I'd been playing since as long as I could talk, and somehow, it all disappeared.

Shit, shit, shit.

"And tonight, performing their number one hit, 'Rooftop Nights,' it's Cosmere!"

The audience cheered. Santi brought in the drum beat for the opening notes. A settling sound. An intro that I'd heard time and time again. And suddenly, I was back in Lubbock at LBK Studios last summer, playing the opening with Campbell for the first time. Both of us knowing that the song was special. A song about meeting Blaire on the Fourth of July that turned into an upbeat hit that no one could get out of their heads, least of all us. And it was that, that got my fingers moving.

The audience disappeared. No one was watching. We were just jamming, as we had been for the last year. I let loose into the keys, pushing my seat back and leaning forward into the keyboard. Campbell's smooth lyrics hit every note bigger and better than he ever had in the studio. It was like we were unleashed. A downpour after a drought.

And through it all, I realized that I wanted this more than ever. I'd never come back from this. Never come down from this.

I'd sell my soul to the music industry to get to feel like this every day.

A smile broke onto my face, and I performed the song like never before.

20

NORA

Weston playing on that stage was like watching someone find religion.

And I understood.

I'd seen Campbell play thousands of times. All growing up, through his years before Cosmere, and then as a mega superstar. I'd known on some level that this was what he had been made for. That he had always known that music spoke to his soul.

But I hadn't gotten it until I saw West transform on that stage. He shed all his other personas, all the ones that had held him back, and he became exactly what I'd seen in Campbell all those years. Despite all the nerves and misgivings, I could see him come alive.

"Wow," I whispered.

"Yeah," Blaire said from my side.

"This is the best I've ever seen them," English agreed.

Anna English was Blaire's publicist. But with the Cosmere publicist, Barbara, out on maternity leave, she had stepped in temporarily for their East Coast performances. She was a New York local and Campbell's friend.

Blaire's hands were clasped together and drawn up to her chest. "I can't believe this came out of one kiss on a rooftop."

English threw an arm around her shoulders. "Believe it, sister. The muse answers when it's called."

Three minutes and forty-five seconds later, the song was over. The crowd exploded with fervor at hearing Cosmere perform. The host came out to congratulate them, shaking hands with Campbell. Then, they went to commercial, the lights turned on, and everything returned to reality.

The band headed back over to the backstage area, as if walking on clouds. Blaire pressed a kiss onto Campbell's lips. Weston moved to my side, and I gave up holding back. I threw my arms around him.

"You were incredible!"

He laughed and hugged me back, swinging me in a quick circle before depositing me on my feet. "Thanks, Snickers."

"Why didn't you *tell* me?"

"Tell you what?"

His eyes dipped to my lips, and I caught my breath. Wondering if we were going to give up this charade. But he pulled back at the last second.

"How magnificent you are."

He ran a hand back through his hair and shot me a self-deprecating smile. "That is not a word I'd ever use to describe me."

"Well, you didn't just see you out there. You were

wonderful. I've seen you play at home, but fuck, West."

His smile was genuine there, if not a little abashed. "Thanks, Nor. That means a lot."

"Come on, you crazy kids," Santi cheered. "Let's go get drunk. We've earned it."

"What he said," Viv agreed.

"I know just the place," English said.

Campbell stayed back for a few more minutes to thank the host, and then we all piled into an awaiting limo outside of Rockefeller Plaza. Though it was only a mile to Percy Tower, with traffic, it took us a solid twenty minutes to navigate the city. Then, we were escorted the back way into the prestigious hotel and swept up into a private elevator.

"My friend actually owns the building," English said. "I called him and asked him to secure us some space in the VIP section."

Weston and I exchanged glances full of incredulity.

But it was Blaire who blurted out, "You know Camden Percy?"

English laughed. "He's the best man in my upcoming wedding."

"Who is Camden Percy?" Viv asked, tapping her lime-green nails on her lips.

"CEO of Percy Enterprise," English said.

"And is he available?" Viv continued.

We all laughed at her audacity, and Santi nudged her.

"He is not," English said with a sly grin. "And don't let his wife hear you say that. I love her to death, but she'd eat you alive if you looked at him funny. Katherine Van Pelt is not to be trifled with."

The elevator opened on the top floor of the hotel to the rooftop bar, Club 360. A bouncer nodded at English as she swept inside with the band, and we were directed to our own private booth in the VIP section. I understood the name of the place now. There was a three-hundred-sixty-degree view of New York City from the top of this skyscraper. We had our own bartender, so no need to go to the bar at the other side of the room, across the already-packed dance floor.

I took the seat next to West as shots were ordered to celebrate their success tonight. We all raised our glasses, and Campbell yelled, "To the new number one song!"

We all cheered and tossed back the shot. The tequila burned all the way down. I nearly choked on it as I scrambled for a lime.

"Whoa," I whispered. "I am way too used to beer."

West laughed. "Yeah. You should take it easy. We don't want you to get sloppy and start crawling around on the floor."

My eyes widened. I shot a furtive look at the group. "You wouldn't want that?"

He winked at me. "All right. Maybe. But not sloppy."

"Maybe?" I asked.

"Definitely." He leaned forward, whispering into my ear, "And have you lie out for me to look, but this time, I get to touch, too."

My cheeks flushed. I'd been so embarrassed by how I'd acted that first night, and now, I wanted nothing more to go back to that moment with him right this very second.

"Not fair," I said. "We can't do anything here."

"Later," he said with a wink.

Then, he stood and headed over to a beckoning Santi. Blaire caught my eye and raised her eyebrows in question. I opened and closed my mouth. What could I say? I needed to be more careful if I didn't want anyone to notice what was going on. Two weeks of incredible sex made it hard to keep my hands to myself.

"Ladies and gentlemen, the party has arrived!"

Our party glanced up at the announcement as a guy strode into our midst with his friends trailing behind him. He was...gorgeous. There was no other way to describe it. He had the build of someone who had never had a moment's pause to his importance. Money dripped off his designer suit and in every self-confident stride forward. And though I'd never seen him before in my life, he looked so much like Blaire's ex, Nate King, that I had to do a double take.

English got to her feet and was swept into a hug. "Gavin King. Since when are you the life of the party?"

"Always, babe," he said, kissing her cheek.

"Fuck off, King." The guy behind him shoved him out of the way and then took English up in his arms and pressed a long, lingering kiss on her lips. He was also almost-unrealistically handsome. I was used to being surrounded by the Wright wealth and prestige in Texas, but this was a whole other world of beauty.

"My fiancé, Court Kensington," English introduced to the rest of the party.

I gaped. "Wait, you're marrying a Kensington? *The* Kensington?"

Court's mother was the mayor of New York City. I'd

seen their engagement photos all over. I hadn't put together that she was *that* Anna English. And now, I was trying not to fangirl. This wedding was a wedding planner's dream.

English grinned. "That's me."

"You're the wedding of the season. All the magazines are talking about it." I was gushing, and still, I couldn't help it.

"See, love, all the magazines are talking about it," Court said with a wink at his fiancée.

She sighed heavily. "Obviously. I know what I'm doing. That doesn't mean I have to be happy about it."

"If you say one more word about eloping," Court warned with a note of humor.

"Please, just be more like your brother." She fluttered her eyelashes at him.

He snagged her in for a rough kiss. "I'll get you for that later."

English laughed and turned back to me. "You follow weddings?"

"Oh, Nora is a wedding planner," Blaire interjected. "She's planning the Locke-King wedding."

"No shit?" Gavin asked, assessing me from head to toe. "You're planning my cousin Margaret's wedding?"

"I am," I said, keeping my work mask in place to deal with all of this excitement. "It should be beautiful."

"Oh, I know Merritt Locke. I bet the wedding will be glamorous." English assessed me for a minute. "Have you ever done anything in LA or New York?"

I gulped. "I haven't."

"English," Court warned.

"I *hate* my wedding planner," English said, shooting Court a look. "My future mother-in-law picked her out, and she doesn't listen to anything I want. It's only a few months away, and I'm pulling my hair out."

"That's a tough place to be in. She should always listen to you first. It's your wedding, not your mother-in-law's."

English arched an eyebrow at her fiancé. "See!" English assessed me. "Do you have a card?"

I tried not to gape at her. Then, I scrambled into my purse and withdrew a business card. Was this real life? "Here you go."

English looked at it and nodded. "I'll be in contact."

Then, she grabbed her fiancé and headed toward Campbell.

"Did that just happen?" I whispered to Blaire.

She laughed. "Looks like it."

"Well, you're going to be busy if you plan a Kensington wedding," Gavin told me.

"Yeah, she will!" Blaire agreed.

"Are you coming to my cousin's wedding?" Gavin asked Blaire.

She shook her head. "I'm going to be in LA. You'll have to tell Nate that I said hi."

"I'll do that," Gavin said with a smirk.

"It'll be good to see a familiar face when I'm there," I told him.

"Yeah, I just need a date."

His eyes passed over Blaire to the girl who had bypassed Gavin to sit with a redhead. She was nearly as short as I was with lavender hair and an effervescent smile. Until Gavin looked at her. Then, it dropped, and she quickly averted her gaze.

There must be a story there.

"And who wouldn't want to go with Gavin King?" Blaire asked.

The last member of their group dropped a hand on Gavin's shoulder and laughed, overhearing our conversation. "Gavin doesn't have a problem finding girls, just keeping them."

Gavin clapped a hand to his chest. "Sam, you wound me."

"Just ask Whitley to go with you," Sam said, gesturing to the lavender-haired girl.

"In what universe would she want to go with me?"

"She was in LA for almost three years," Sam said. "A lot can change in three years."

Blaire and I exchanged a look. "Sounds like a story," Blaire said.

Gavin sighed heavily, as if resigned to what was about to happen.

Sam arched an eyebrow at him and then explained, "He and Whitley had a fling a few years back when she and her boyfriend were broken up. She got back with her boyfriend, and he found out they'd hooked up. It was a huge blowup in the middle of Fashion Week."

"I wouldn't do that to Robert."

"Robert is seeing someone else. Happily. And he doesn't blame you anymore," Sam interjected with a pointed look.

"I say, go for it," Blaire said. "That sounds like a lot of wasted time."

I bit my lip. I knew the feeling of betrayal in all of this. I'd experienced it myself. But three years was a long time to hold on to that feeling, and it was clear to me in Gavin's look that he still felt something for Whitley.

"Definitely," I agreed. "I'll look out for you at the wedding."

Gavin's eyes strayed back to Whitley, as if he could will her to look at him. "We'll see."

That was the end of that conversation. The song shifted, and English was there, pulling everyone out onto the dance floor. I laughed as Blaire grabbed me and took me with her. I let loose in the crush of it all. I'd never been much of a dancer, but it was liberating with so many people all in one place.

Then, I felt hands on my hips. I gasped, ready to scold whoever was touching me, but a mouth was at my ear. "It's me."

I relaxed back against West. There were so many people, but still, not enough to completely hide that we were dancing this close. That our movements were perfectly synced, as if we'd worked overtime at night to synchronize our bodies. But no one seemed to care that we were this close. No one paid any attention at all.

And for this night, I forgot about the potential consequences to our entanglement and let myself pretend that this was forever. It was a dangerous thought. A thrilling idea. One I shouldn't want this bad.

Yet I couldn't lie to myself and say I didn't want Weston Wright.

21

WESTON

We closed the bar down with English's friends.

I was just past tipsy, but Campbell was as drunk as I'd ever seen him. It was only because of Blaire all but holding him up that he made it back to his room at all. The rest of the band headed to our rooms in Percy Tower.

Nora waved at us. She'd stopped drinking hours ago, and she was the steadiest on her feet compared to everyone else. "Night, y'all."

"Night, Nora," Viv said, blowing her a kiss as Nora opened her door.

Nora's gaze shifted to me before she disappeared into the room.

Viv wrapped an arm around my shoulders. "Hey now, don't let Campbell see you doing that."

"Doing what?" I asked, suddenly nervous.

"Looking at his sister like she's a tasty snack."

Santi laughed. "She is though. I'd hit that if I didn't think Campbell would skewer me."

"Hey," a girl said on Santi's arm.

"I mean that in the best way, babe," Santi said.

Yorke snorted. "Yeah."

Santi opened the door for the girl to go in with him, which she did despite his stupidity. Viv winked at me as she got to her room. Yorke held up two fingers in good-bye. Both of them disappeared, and then it was just me. I could go back into my room at the end of the hall if I wanted.

Or...

I took two steps backward and crept back to Nora's room. I knocked twice gently.

She cracked the door open. "About time."

Her hand fell onto the front my shirt, yanking me inside. The door crashed closed behind me, my hands tangled in her hair, and our mouths collided.

"Fuck," I groaned, tasting this fucking girl.

"You are such a tease." She kissed me harder, deeper. "Your hands on me all night. Your hips against mine. Your body so hot."

My hands moved exactly where she'd mentioned, tugging her harder against me. "I wanted you."

"It's hard to stay away."

"So hard," I said, thrusting forward.

Her fingers deftly moved down the buttons of my shirt, pulling the bottom loose from my pants.

"Not fair," she said, running her nails down my abs. "Not fair at all."

Then, she was removing my belt, dragging the zipper down low, and dropping to her knees before me. I went utterly still as I watched her yank my pants down my hips and remove my cock from my boxers.

She stroked me up and down in her hand. Gone was the girl uncertain with herself. Here she was, the firecracker I'd always seen her as. The girl she'd been before someone tried to blow out her flame. Two weeks of incredible sex later, and no longer would I hear her say that she couldn't come from sex, that she was difficult, or any of those other ridiculous things.

Only the heartthrob I'd known was in there.

"Now, who isn't being fair?" I groaned as she licked up the seam at the head.

She grinned devilishly. "Oh, did you want something?"

Before I could answer, she took my cock in her mouth. I moaned, pushing my fingers into her hair as she took me in deeper.

"Fuck, fuck, fuck," I muttered.

Then, she moved, dragging out and bobbing back down on me. I watched her enjoyment as she sucked me. She'd been hesitant about this, too. It had only been used as a guilt trip in the past, and now, she was here, offering it to me on her knees. She had come a long way. And I fucking adored it.

She worked more vigorously at my cock, sliding her hand up and down the shaft. Most of the time, I'd let her get me off like this, but not tonight. I needed to be inside of her. I needed her little body.

"Snickers," I said, drawing her back off me.

"I wasn't finished."

"You said you'd crawl for me."

Her eyes widened. She'd said it in jest, and I thought she might tell me to go fuck myself. But then, to my amazement, she dropped to her hands, gave me a filthy look as she glanced back at me, and then crawled toward the bed. Her skirt this evening was *not* flouncy, as it had been that first night. And as she moved away from me, it rode up her hips and exposed every inch of her ass, including the bright red thong.

"God, that's a sight."

She made it onto the bed and flopped backward, not bothering to tug down her dress. "Well, you looked. Are you going to come touch?"

"Fuck yes."

I ripped off my pants as she removed her dress and thong. Then, I snagged her hips and wrenched her down on the bed toward me. She squeaked and then laughed softly. I flipped her over onto all fours.

She pushed her ass back toward me. "Please."

The word undid me. I hastily sheathed myself before plunging deep inside of her. She gasped and reached back to grab my hand.

"So full," she murmured.

"Take me all the way," I encouraged, pulling out and thrusting again. It took a few thrusts before she opened fully enough for me to seat myself inside of her.

I took the one hand she'd offered, her face pressing into the comforter, and then I grabbed the other. I drew her wrists together into one hand to use as leverage as I withdrew and then shot back inside of her.

She gasped. "Fuck."

"Yes," I cried out.

I'd been close with her lips wrapped around my cock. I'd been so close that it was almost painful to stop. But I wanted to finish inside of her. Her moans of pleasure as I kept up a fast rhythm told me all I needed to know about what she wanted, too.

"Come with me," I commanded.

I thrust harder, the sounds of wet skin smacking together over and over. She shouted her orgasm into the mattress. With her pussy tight around me, I came hard, roaring into the bedroom. Heedless of who heard.

"Oh God, oh God, oh God," she said. "Wow."

I released her arms and rubbed an encouraging hand down her spine. "You were perfect."

She shivered as I pulled out of her, collapsing into a heap on the bed. I discarded the condom into a trash bin. Then, I wrapped myself around her.

"West," she whispered.

"Hmm?"

She yawned. "You probably can't sleep here."

"I won't," I told her.

"But I want you to."

"I know." I kissed her shoulder and banded my arm across her stomach to pull her in closer. "I don't have to leave yet."

She yawned again. "Okay."

I held her in my arms as my mind began to drift. Tonight had been incredible. Easily one of the best nights of my life. I'd never thought I'd get to play that sort of venue where millions watched on. And then to end it here, like this. It was more than I could have dreamed. In fact, I imagined for a second what it would be like to have Nora with me all the time in LA.

Except it was a fantasy, not reality. Because Campbell would never be okay with this. And Nora couldn't just leave Lubbock. Her entire life was there. We were lucky that she hadn't already had a wedding this weekend.

And with that bout of disappointment, I circled back to what had been bugging me all night—my dad.

He'd called. He was proud of me. And yet...and yet... he was a supreme asshole. How could I reconcile wanting his approval and despising him for everything he'd done to me?

Nora's breathing began to slow, and I could feel her slipping toward unconsciousness. "Nora?"

She startled at my voice. "Hmm?"

I didn't know how to bring this up. I'd never talked about the complications with my dad with anyone but my siblings. People who understood. Even Jordan and Julian didn't really understand. How could they?

"My dad called before the show."

She slowly rolled over and looked up into my eyes. "I didn't think y'all were talking."

"We're not. Well, Whitt told me that he wanted to congratulate me."

"And did he?"

"Yeah, he did." I sighed. "Which is all I ever wanted from him."

"But?" she asked, as if hearing the hesitation in my voice.

"I don't trust him. I don't believe him. Is he really

happy for me, or is he going to use it as an excuse to get back in and hurt me?"

"I don't know," she said softly. "I'm not sure you'd know without talking to him, but for what it's worth, I think he is proud of you."

"Yeah? Why is that?"

"Because look at you," she said. "You're taking over the world. You played *The Tonight Show*. It's a lot. I'm proud of you."

Her words had the desired effect of making my chest warm. Her approval made me nearly as happy as my father's.

"Thank you."

She leaned forward and pressed a kiss to my lips. "What are you afraid of?"

I closed my eyes. "That I'm just like him."

"You're not..."

"You're a secret," I blurted out.

She put her hands on my face. "Look at me."

I did as she'd asked. I hated comparing myself to him. But how could I not? Was I doing the same shit he had, so I could get what I wanted?

"It's not the same," she said.

"Isn't it?"

She laughed and shook her head. "You're not hiding me because you're married to someone else. Wait, are you?"

I laughed and shook my head. "But..."

"We agreed to this."

"My mom must have agreed, too."

"West, you're leaving after all of this. You're going

back to LA, permanently. This isn't a way for you to have your cake and eat it too. If you were doing that, you'd string me along. You'd make me believe that this could work when you were gone. You'd get to have me when you could have me, and you'd have whoever you wanted in LA, too."

I cringed at that thought. "I'd never do that," I said with vehemence.

She smiled. "I know. That's the point. You're not like him." She threaded our fingers together. "It's hard. All of it is hard. I know all about hard. I lost my mom when I was fourteen. Then, Campbell left for LA the following year. Hollin was in college. It was just me and Dad, and he was grieving. So, it felt like it was I was all alone. We're all close now, but we're still recovering from the wound that her absence left behind."

"Growing up like that must have been difficult,."

"It was isolating. My brothers weren't around much, but just enough to scare off any boys who might have shown interest. My dad was a shell for the first year, and by the time he started noticing me again, he became super protective as well. I wasn't always close with my mom, but life would have been different with her still here. Sometimes, I feel guilty, thinking life would have been better. That I would have had some defense against everyone's protective instincts."

"You shouldn't feel guilty about that. Of course you want your mom back."

She pressed a kiss to my lips. "We're both a little fucked up, aren't we?"

I chuckled. "Did you have a childhood if you aren't?"

"Fair. What are you going to do about your dad?"

I sighed heavily and rolled onto my back. She snuggled in close, laying her head on my chest.

"I don't know."

"You don't have to decide today. Just leave the door open. You'll know what to do when the time is right."

"Thanks, Nor," I said, running my fingers back through her hair.

"Of course."

Her breathing slowed again, and then when I was sure that she was asleep, I reluctantly withdrew. I looked down at this beautiful girl and wondered if she was right. Was I really nothing like my dad? Because at times, I felt like I was following in his footsteps, and I hated myself for it.

I headed back to my room alone. I'd almost fallen asleep when I'd been at Nora's side. Now, I stared up at the ceiling, wishing for that same comfort and finding none of it.

22

NORA

Waking up alone in that hotel room made me sad. I'd told West that none of it mattered. In fact, I basically convinced him that this was all peachy. I hadn't wanted him to think that he was like his dad. Because he wasn't.

And still, I'd been sad when I woke up.

I'd agreed to all of this. I wanted that fun fling since I'd never done anything like this before in my life. But I wasn't supposed to develop real feelings. I wasn't supposed to have feelings about him being gone from my bed.

Not that I planned to tell him that. He was stressed enough with the band and now his dad. We were having fun for the few weeks before he went back to LA. This didn't have to be complicated.

It would be better when we returned home. We lived together, so there was less sneaking. I could wake up in his bed any day of the week if I wanted. And I did most nights of the week. He spent a lot of time at the condo

Campbell had purchased in town, going over stuff for the album release.

I could feel the clock ticking on our tryst.

It was easy not to think about it, considering wedding season was in full swing. Jordan and Annie's wedding had basically kicked off my busy season. I was at work from sunup until sundown almost every night. Every Friday and Saturday night and even some Sunday afternoons, there were local weddings at Wright Vineyard. The only thing I had time for other than my job was crashing into West's bed at night and soccer on Sunday nights.

"I'm going to be late," I grumbled as I strode into the house on my four-inch high heels.

"We still have time," West said. He was playing a video game in the living room but gave up as I ran into my bedroom to change into my soccer uniform.

The Tacos were playing the indoor soccer championship tonight, but my wedding had run late, and thus *I* was running late for the game. Fewer players played on an indoor pitch, but Annie had been called in to the ER unexpectedly, Cézanne hadn't been able to play all season, and Eve had a house to show, so she wouldn't make it until the second half.

Which meant, without me, they would be playing a man down. In the championship.

"Just imagine if I could work less," I said as I tugged my shirt over my head and snatched up my bag. I threw him the keys to my truck.

"You *could* work less," he said.

I almost growled at him. That was how little downtime I had. "I could, but I don't know how not to hustle."

"I get it. It's hard when you're following your dream job." I scoffed, and he glanced over at me in surprise as we got into the truck. "What? Wright Vineyard isn't your dream job?"

"*Dream* implies something I fantasize about. What person fantasizes about working a hundred hours a week from April to October?"

"Fair. What would your dream job be then?"

"If I had my pick...I'd work a handful of fabulous weddings a year. I'd get these incredible, outrageously expensive weddings, and my fee would cover my expenses for the rest of the year. Then, I could travel the world. I mean, even getting to go away during the summer would be nice."

"That does sound like a dream."

I sighed and kicked my feet up on the dash. "Not that it seems likely."

"You never heard from English?"

I frowned and looked down at my clasped hands. I'd told West about that interaction in New York City. He'd been excited for the opportunity for me, but it wasn't like she'd been serious. "No. I haven't heard from her. She was probably in the moment."

"Maybe."

"Anyway, I need to tell Hollin that we need to hire someone else. We could bring Tessi on full-time and get a few more assistants since the wedding business has burgeoned so dramatically."

"Do that," he said automatically. "I don't like to see you this stressed."

"I'd be less stressed if I wasn't going to be late to this game."

"We're going to make it," Weston said. "And I called Harley earlier when you said you'd be late. She played in high school. She was excited to cover for you. She might already be there."

I blew out a breath of relief. That did make me feel better. But I detested being late for *anything*.

West's phone beeped as we turned off the loop toward the indoor complex. "That's Harley. She said she's there. Isaac gave her Annie's uniform. So, you can breathe."

"Fine. Fine. But it's the championship game."

He reached across the dash and took my hand. "It'll be fine."

"With my luck, Harley will be better than me, and they won't want to sub me in."

I wasn't *that* bad, but I'd only gotten into soccer for The Tacos. Originally because August was so good at soccer that he wanted to play on Hollin's team. I'd agreed and worked hard to be good enough to be on the team. I'd once told Hollin that my breakup with August was worse for the team, and he'd scolded me. Not because I was better than August, but because we had gotten Eve out of the situation, and she was *way* better than him.

Still, I didn't want to miss the final game of the indoor season.

West pulled into the parking lot three minutes after the game started. My fuzzy pink dice swinging dangerously from the rearview window.

"We made good time," I said, dropping out of the

passenger seat and hurrying around to the driver's side to grab my bag from the back.

West stepped out next to me. "Before you go." He snagged my arm, pulling me toward him.

"I don't have time."

"I know," he said as he pushed my back against the SUV.

My heart rate accelerated as he took control of my body. His lips descended on mine, and I gave in, wrapping my arms around his neck and letting him kiss me breathless. He was distracting me from my nerves in the same way I'd done for him in New York City. He could kiss me here without anyone around to see.

And I wanted this. God, I wanted this.

The kiss turned feverish, and for one delirious moment, I wondered if we had time for a quickie in the parking lot. It couldn't possibly happen. Not with the game beckoning. But it was a glorious fantasy.

"West," I groaned.

"I know. I know. You have to go."

"I really do."

And then I kissed him again for good measure.

The crunch of gravel under feet should have been the indication that someone was getting nearer, but I was lost to West's lips.

It wasn't until a throat cleared and someone said, "Nora?" that I pulled back.

I'd know that voice anywhere.

"August?" I gasped in surprise.

He froze, looking between me and West in shock. He saw straight through what was happening here. West's arm was still around my waist. My back braced against the SUV. I stumbled forward.

I didn't have to justify myself. August had hurt me in the worst way possible. He'd demolished my heart and then kept right on rolling over it. He had no right to look at me as if I were the person doing something wrong.

"What are you doing here?" I forced out.

"I...I came to talk to you." He glanced back toward the indoor facility. "I knew you'd be at the championship game."

"And why would you think I'd want to talk to you? I told you that I didn't want to see you anymore. Multiple times actually."

He nodded. His eyes shifting to West, who still had said nothing, and back to me. "Can we have a moment...alone?"

"That doesn't sound like a good idea," I said at the same time West growled, "No."

I put my hand on his chest to stop him. I could handle this. I could handle August.

"I said all I needed to say to you. Go back to your fiancée," I said with venom in my voice.

He swallowed. "I see."

"I don't think you do. I'm not the same girl that you abused, August," I told him.

"Abused?" he asked in a straggled gasp. "Nora, I would never..."

"The woman said what she said," Weston said.

"Why don't you stay out of this?" August snapped at him.

"I don't think I have to do that. You heard her." West

straightened to his considerable height and crossed his arms over his chest. "She doesn't want anything to do with you."

August looked ready to argue, but since when did he fight for what he wanted? When had he ever fought for me? No, he gave me one more pleading look and then slunk away.

"I have no idea what that was about."

West shook his head. "He's up to something."

"Well, whatever it is, I don't want any part of it."

"Good," he said, pressing a kiss to my hair.

I wasn't sure he even realized that he'd done it. How intimate it was. It wasn't about sex…or anything with our little fling. It was just what he'd wanted in that moment. I glanced up at him, and my stomach flipped at the look still on his face. The one that said he'd do anything to keep me from being hurt by that ass again.

But who was going to protect my heart from him?

23

WESTON

A few days later, my fingers flew across the piano. I was lost in the music, humming the lyrics I'd put to my beat. It wasn't something that Cosmere would ever sing. Those were exclusively Campbell's songs, but this was something else. Something important to me.

And something I could currently drive all my anxiety about said band into.

"I like that," a voice said from behind me.

I cut off playing and found Nora in the doorway to my music room. She was in a white dress with green flowers on it and nude high heels. She leaned her hip against the doorframe and crossed her arms. She'd been swamped with work, and I'd hardly seen her since the championship.

"You're home early," I noted.

"Tessi started full-time yesterday. She told me to take the afternoon off," she explained as she walked over to my upright piano.

"Thank God for Tessi."

I reached for her, pulling her down into my lap. She laughed but settled into place as I played the simplified chords of the song.

"You've played that for me before, haven't you?"

"I have." I pressed a kiss into her shoulder. "It's your song."

She startled. "*My* song?"

"Uh-huh," I said, moving smoothly up the keys and then back down. "I call it 'Nora's Melody.' "

Her cheeks flushed. "I didn't know I had my own melody."

"Just something I've been working on."

All the tension left her body, and we sat there, not speaking. I let the music speak for itself. Said all the things about her that I couldn't get into words. The things that were too tangled up with the fact that I was going back to LA. And that we had an expiration date. Still, I couldn't stop thinking about her. I couldn't stop writing about her.

"It's beautiful," she whispered, swiping at her eye. "I've never had a song written about me. Does it have lyrics?"

I shrugged. "Something I'm still working on. The keys are easier for me than words. I've always understood the music."

"I can tell. It almost doesn't need words."

I moved back up the keys as I came toward the conclusion. When I landed on middle C, the note long and mournful, I pulled my hands back and wrapped my arms around her.

"Can we stay like this?"

She dropped her head back and tilted it to look at me. "If only."

I drew her mouth to me, pressing down firmly. "What's your plan for today? A whole afternoon off."

"I'm not sure. I was thinking of going to see Apple."

I blinked at her. "Apple?"

She laughed. "She owns the nursery I frequent. She's probably confused as to why she hasn't seen me in months."

"Of course you're on a first-name basis with the nursery owner."

"You'd like her."

"I think you're right."

"You could come with me."

I arched an eyebrow at her. "What do I need with a plant?"

She came to her feet and rolled her eyes at me. "What? Would you rather mope in this room the rest of the day?"

"Ouch."

She wasn't wrong. I had been moping. I'd been moping all week since Campbell had gone back to LA without me. He said he had some stuff to work out with the band. I offered to go with him, but he said that he didn't need me. And I'd tried not to flinch at those words.

They'd needed me for so long. Michael had left the band, and I was the one who had stepped up to make sure Campbell's vision was realized. I'd recorded with them. I'd played with them in New York City. And now, I wasn't needed. It brought out the darker side of my personality to know that my art had been good enough, and now, it wasn't.

Nora had told me that wasn't at all the case, and a part of me knew that she was right. I was self-aware enough to know that I was dealing with imposter syndrome. It didn't make any of it any easier.

She dropped her hands to my shoulders. "I'm sorry. I didn't mean it like that. You're just so sad."

My hands returned to her hips, drawing her back into me. "I'm an artist. Sad is when I work best."

"I guess so. I don't like to see you like this."

"And a plant will fix it?"

She laughed and nodded. "It works for me."

"You've convinced me."

I stood, taking her with me. She yelped and then wrapped her legs around my waist. I carried her into my room, tossing her gently back onto my bed.

"This does not feel like going to get a plant."

"Priorities," I said as I ran my hands up her inner thighs and pressed my mouth against her underwear.

She gasped out, "West!"

Fuck, I loved to hear that.

I tugged her panties off and buried my face between her legs. She tasted like fucking heaven. I'd had a rough couple of days. She'd been gone a lot. I needed to find salvation here with her.

Her fingers threaded through my hair, which had grown long enough to pull. I groaned against her body as she did just that.

"Fuck."

She came on my mouth a few minutes later in a

panting mess. I loved to see her this way. I still could hardly believe that someone had convinced her she couldn't come like this. I'd never understand it since she was so utterly responsive with me.

I rolled a condom on and then pulled her down on top of me.

She laughed. "This is what you want?"

I maneuvered my cock, aligning it with her awaiting pussy. Then, she settled down inch after inch until I was seated inside of her. She braced her hands on my chest and made a soft noise. Her eyes were closed and her mouth slightly open. She looked like a fucking painting. I wanted to mark this in my memory forever.

I grasped her hips and rolled them back and forth.

"That is..." she stammered. "Oh...oh God."

"Close again already?" I teased.

She shot me a look as she lifted her hips and dropped back down onto me. "Are you?"

I dug my fingers into her hips at the sheer perfection of her. Then, I worked her up and slammed her down over and over again. She braced herself forward as everything built and built and built.

"Fuck," I cried out.

"Yes."

I was so close. And then she pressed us together, chest to chest, just moving her hips up and down. The contact made me unleash. I cried out as I came inside of her. She made mewling noises as she clenched tight all around me. Then, her body went limp.

"I should come home early more often," she murmured with a sigh as she rolled off me.

I chuckled softly. "I will not disagree."

After tossing the condom, I changed into jeans and a T-shirt. Nora was pulling her panties back on when I turned around. I hadn't even gotten her out of her dress. We were a little more rumpled than when we'd started.

I snagged the keys from Nora and drove her SUV south. She didn't seem to mind anymore that I'd started driving her around. I loved my Subaru, but her CR-V was newer with fewer miles. And I felt safer behind the wheel than as her passenger. To say she was a reckless driver was an understatement. Sometimes, I wondered how she'd passed her driver's test.

"There it is," she said with excitement shining on her face.

Apple's Nursery was sort of a hole-in-the-wall. She'd mentioned the place in passing, but I'd never seen it before. It was a small building tucked onto the end of a strip mall with a greenhouse on one end, but Nora looked at it as if it were El Dorado.

She grabbed my hand and all but skipped toward the entrance. "Come on."

Her enthusiasm was infectious. I could feel my bad mood sliding off of me. Somehow, she was always able to get me out of these depressive episodes. I didn't know how she knew exactly what I needed, but she did.

A bell dinged overhead when we entered. There were a half-dozen patrons already inside, browsing the dense selection of greenery that took up every inch of the place. It smelled fresh and earthy inside. It was...settling. I'd lived the last couple months surrounded by Nora's plants, and this felt nice. I wasn't sure how I'd lived my whole life without a houseful of plants. Though I probably would have killed them all, but Nora managed to effortlessly keep them all alive. Green thumb on that one.

"Well, what do I do?"

"You pick a plant," she said with a laugh.

"But how do I know which one to get?"

She shrugged. "Talk to them."

I blinked at her, waiting to see if she was joking. She wasn't. "I...talk to them?"

"Yeah. How else do you find out if you're going to be friends?"

"You're insane."

She laughed. "A little. Just go wander around and see if any of them speak back. I'm going to say hi to Apple."

She scampered off toward the register, and I headed down the aisles, feeling a little bit foolish. I wasn't sure what to say to any of the plants. Did talking to them really help?

I tried it on a few plants and felt even *more* foolish. A couple looked at me oddly when they found me trying to say hello to a fern. I hurried away, wondering if this was some alarming prank Nora had laid on me. But she hadn't come back. So, I continued to walk the shelving.

Then, I came in front of a small potted cactus. It was spiky and imperfect. The lone cactus on the shelf.

"All alone, too?" I asked it.

A prickly loner felt all too familiar.

I picked up the cactus and waited to see if it would talk back, as Nora had mentioned. I felt dumb, but somehow, it almost felt like it did. I tucked it under my arm, careful not to prick myself on one of its spikes, and then walked to the register.

Nora stood, speaking animatedly with an older woman with round cheeks and a kind smile. "Oh, here he is. Did you find something?"

I held up the cactus. "This one."

Nora's lips quirked up. "He's adorable."

"Good choice," the woman said.

"West, this is Apple. Apple, Weston Wright."

"So good to meet you," Apple said pleasantly. "It's nice to meet the man that my Nora has been gushing about."

I flushed slightly at that comment. "Nice to meet you, ma'am."

"Ma'am," Apple said, glancing at Nora. "I like this one."

Nora grinned. "Me too."

"Ah, young love," she mused, taking the cactus out of my arm.

I sputtered at that word. *Love.* Nora met my eyes, and then we both quickly looked away. We hadn't said that word. I mean...I was *leaving*. I was going back to LA. That word would only ruin everything we had right now. It didn't matter how I felt. Not truly. Because even if nothing worked out with Campbell and Cosmere, then I was still going to take the producing job.

"Apple," Nora admonished, "we're just roommates."

"Bah!" she said. "You young people and your labels. Back in my day, if you looked at each other the way that you two do, you'd be past dating and halfway to engaged."

Nora laughed. "That's not really how it's done anymore."

"So I've heard. It sounds exhausting and complicated."

Couldn't fault her there. It was complicated.

Before Nora could say anything else, her phone started to ring. She looked down at it with alarm. "Uh, excuse me for a minute."

She took a few steps away, but I didn't miss the name she uttered incredulously. "Tamara?"

"She's special, you know?" Apple said as she handed me the receipt for my new cactus.

"I do know."

Apple arched an eyebrow. "Do you?"

"Yes."

"Because it looks like you're going to let the best thing to happen to you slip through your fingers like the last idiot who hurt her."

I gaped at her. "I promise you, ma'am, I have no intention of hurting her."

She guffawed at me. "No one intends to hurt someone. They just do it."

I didn't know what to say to that. Guilt settled into the pit of my stomach. I had something special here, but I had something special in LA, too. I didn't see a way that I could possibly have both.

"You let that girl know how you feel before it's too late," Apple added.

I gulped and nodded. Before it was too late. When was that? Fuck.

Nora's voice rose. "I don't have to listen to this!"

Then, she hung up and strode back toward me like a thundercloud. "Let's go."

"What happened?"

She shook her head and controlled her expression enough to give Apple a hug and tell her good-bye. By the time we got back to her truck, she had clouded over again.

"Nora," I said, grabbing her arm. "Talk to me."

She sighed heavily, deflating like a balloon. "August broke off the engagement."

I froze at those words. The careful delivery, as if she had no emotions about them. But I could hear how brittle she'd sounded underneath it. I hadn't heard that from her in so long. I hated the way it had come out.

I wanted to punch August so bad right now. He'd better not fucking think this was his way back in because that wasn't fucking happening.

"Really?"

"Yes, Tamara called to congratulate me."

"Whatever for?"

I held my breath, feeling like I'd created a prophecy and it was about to come true.

She met my gaze with a look, like she was drowning. "Because apparently, he told her he still loved me."

24

NORA

August still loved me.

Ice snapped under my feet, dragging me beneath a freezing pond. I felt chilled to the bone at those words.

All that work I'd done to get over him. All that time I'd wanted nothing more than to not feel like this anymore. Everything I'd been through because of him. And now—*now*—he claimed to still love me?

"And...how do you feel about that?" West asked carefully.

So carefully. Too carefully.

I wanted to reassure him. I wanted to tell him that I felt nothing about it. But it would be a lie. I'd thought I'd moved on completely, but first love stuck with you. I knew what August and I had was never ever going to be the same. How could I forgive him for what he'd done? Saying he was in love with me didn't flip a switch.

I shook my head and looked away. "I don't know."

"Nora..."

He reached for me, and I let him drag me against him. Tears came to my eyes, unbidden. I hated it. I hated them. I'd told myself I was done crying over August. I was so far past done.

"It's okay," West said. "It must be confusing."

"I wanted him to love me, to choose me for so long, West."

His body tensed at those words. How hard it must be for him to comfort me when I was upset about another man. But still, he said, "It's okay. Your feelings are real."

"No," I said, pulling back and swiping at my tears. "That's not what I mean. I don't still love him. I just...I loved him for so long. But he didn't choose me. He didn't love me when I needed him to."

"No, he didn't," West agreed.

I straightened and hardened, as if I were shoring up all the cracks in my foundation. "He doesn't get to choose to miraculously love me again. That's not how it works. He cheated on me. He proposed to someone else."

"And then he saw us together at the soccer game."

My face lit up with recognition. "You don't think..."

"That he was jealous? Yeah, I do," West said confidently.

"He wouldn't break off his engagement because he saw us kissing."

"Looks like he just did."

My head swam. That was absurd. All this time, he'd wanted to have his cake and eat it too. He wanted me to pine after him. The way I always returned his feverish texts and met him in the park and played his little game. But when I stopped playing, he decided he wanted me back? It was too coincidental not to be true, and somehow, I found it unfathomable.

He could have had me whenever he wanted me for almost an entire year after I caught him cheating. Now, when he couldn't have me, he wanted me?

"That's terrible. I almost feel bad for Tamara."

West snorted. "Don't. She went into all of this willingly."

"I guess she did."

In fact, I'd always suspected that Tamara had been the aggressor. She'd had little remorse through so much of it. She shoved it in my face that they were engaged. She'd *won*. But still, it couldn't have felt good to hear that. August had hurt us both.

"I just...fuck, I don't know." I ran a hand back through my hair. "I feel like I want to run away."

"Then, let's run away."

I looked up at him warily. "What do you mean?"

"I mean exactly what I said. You need to get out of Lubbock. I'm going crazy, pacing and waiting for Campbell to get back. Let's go do something. What's something you've always wanted to do?"

I shrugged. "Paris."

He laughed. "Okay, maybe something a little closer?"

"Well, I've always wanted to go to White Sands."

"What's that?"

"A national park with white sand dunes. You can sled and hike there. A friend went in college and came back, raving that it was like touching the stars when you were out all alone on the dunes. I've always wanted that. But it's, like, five hours away, and I have to work tomorrow."

"Call out."

My eyebrows hit my forehead. "You're serious?"

"Yeah. Let's go."

I opened my mouth, ready with a quick retort. I couldn't possibly run away in the middle of the week. I had weddings this weekend to deal with. I *always* had weddings to deal with. But maybe this was what I needed.

"Okay."

Less than an hour later, we were heading west, on our way to New Mexico. It was about a five-hour drive, and I snagged a BnB in Alamogordo, the nearest city outside of the dunes. I rearranged my schedule for tomorrow while we drove, moving some meetings to next week, which I was sure I'd hate later. But for now, it felt worth it.

I didn't know why I hadn't anticipated it, but August started calling that night.

West glanced at the name on the phone and pursed his lips. "Are you going to answer that?"

"No," I said automatically.

In fact, I put the phone on silent and didn't look at it the rest of the night. We made use of the double bed, unable to hold back our laughter at the loud creaking noises it made. And then woke up bright and early the next morning, taking his Subaru to the entrance of the park.

We bought sleds and wax at the visitors center and drove into the sea of white dunes. It wasn't actually sand even though it looked like it. The sand was gypsum, which was used commercially in drywall. Thankfully, the gypsum here hadn't been stripped clear, and it was still a beautiful nature preserve. As if we were standing in an endless desert in the middle of New Mexico.

We took our sleds up to the top of an empty dune, waxed it to high heaven, and then proceeded to flop around uselessly.

I laughed myself into hysterics when West made it halfway down and then rolled through the sand face-first. "Oh my God, do that again!"

"I don't know how you're doing it," he grumbled.

"The trick is to lay on your back, so there's more surface area. Your butt just digs into the sand and slows you down."

He eyed me warily as we trudged back up the dune. "Are you calling my butt fat?"

I snorted. "Hardly." I slapped my own ass. "I've got junk in my trunk."

He threw his sled to the ground and picked me up by my ass. I wrapped my arms and legs around him and giggled. We spun in circles until we were dizzy and collapsed into the sand.

West leaned over me, brushing sand off my cheek. "I love this freckle," he said, touching a spot next to my lips.

"Yeah?"

"It's my favorite. Well, you have one right here," he said, pointing to my pelvis. "I like to taste that one right before I taste you."

"Filthy."

He didn't respond; he just kissed me.

Our tongues met and twined, drawing out the gesture

until we were both breathing heavy—and not from trekking up the dunes. Eventually, a family came near us, and we broke apart.

"Let's try again," I said. "You're going to get this."

We set up our sleds on the pathways we'd made, and then together, we pushed off. Both of us flew down the slopes, screaming and whooping as we went.

West crashed at the end, going tumbling. But then he jumped up, holding his sled above his head. "I did it! Let's go again!"

I laughed but couldn't resist his enthusiasm. We ran up and slid down that mountain over and over until we were exhausted and everyone had left us alone again.

Then, we lay side by side at the top of the dune, our fingers interlocked, staring up at the sun. I knew that we had to go back soon. It was a five-hour drive back to Lubbock, and I couldn't play hooky twice this week. But I wasn't ready to let this feeling go.

I wanted to hold on to it gently, like carrying an egg on a spoon.

"It is like touching the stars," West said.

"Like there's no one else in the whole world."

"Just one."

He brought my hand to his and kissed it. My stomach did a somersault. Apple had said we were young love. That it was all too complicated for her. But here, out in the open, it felt so simple.

"West," I said, turning to face him.

His eyes swept to mine. "Yeah?"

I wanted to tell him what I'd been feeling for a long time. That this wasn't just a fling, that it was so much more to me. That I wanted everything with him. Every silent moment, every stolen star.

But when I looked at him, my tongue stuck to the roof of my mouth like peanut butter. I couldn't do it. I couldn't break the spell.

Instead, I kissed him and let him roll me onto my back. The words unspoken as I gave myself to him.

25

WESTON

Getting away for even a day was exactly what Nora had needed. Exactly what I'd needed, too. I'd been obsessing about the band. While out on White Sands, I hadn't thought about it at all. No, it was hard to think of anything but Nora when I was alone with her.

This wasn't supposed to happen. Fuck. What was I even doing?

I was at my piano again two days later when a knock sounded on the door. Nora had a wedding today. She wouldn't be free until late. Whitt was at work...on a Saturday, and Harley was apparently busy. I suspected she was dating someone, and that was why I hadn't seen much of her. I had no idea who would be at my door.

When I opened it, Campbell Abbey was standing in the doorway.

"Hey, man! I didn't know you were back from LA."

"I just got back in. You busy?" Campbell asked.

"Nah, messing around with a new song on the piano."

Campbell's eyes brightened. "A new song? Can I hear?"

Oh shit. Yeah, hadn't thought about that one. "If you want. It's not done."

"You've seen my half-formed shit. Time for you to do the same."

I laughed; I couldn't help it. Campbell was always like that. So self-effacing. As if it weren't strange that we'd become such close friends so fast. I wanted to say he was like this with everyone, but we'd just clicked. Which was why Nora had thought I should just fucking talk to him about the band stuff. Maybe I should finally do that.

"Yeah, sure. Come in. I'll play it for you."

"I got a better idea. Let's lay it down at the studio."

"Here?" I asked in surprise.

"Yeah. Our best material came out of those sessions."

He wasn't wrong, but we hadn't been working on my songs. I'd been matching his material. I didn't know why it felt like a huge difference, but it did.

But it was Campbell. How could I say no?

"Cool."

I'd talk to him about the band while recording. He was always in his best mood when we were there. It was long overdue anyway.

I slid my wallet into my back pocket, grabbed my phone, and headed out to Campbell's Range Rover. He turned on Foo Fighters as we drove toward downtown.

"How was LA?" I asked.

He shrugged. "Same old, same old."

"Yeah."

"Good to be back in Lubbock. Probably the last time for a while."

"Why is that?"

"Album release, press tour, tour," he said, ticking them off on his fingers.

I shot a glance at him, wondering if he was going to say anything else, but he just hummed along to the lyrics. As if none of that bothered him.

"How does Blaire feel about that?"

He grinned. "She's coming with me."

My stomach knotted. How easy it was to have someone who could pick up and go with you anywhere in the world.

"She's going to leave Lubbock?"

"Not forever. She'd miss it too much. So would I actually. Just long-distance is hard. Nearly impossible really, and we can both fly back and forth whenever we want. It'll be nice to have her with me."

I bet it would. I clenched my hand into a fist and looked out the window as Lubbock passed me by. Lubbock wasn't even my home. I'd grown up in Seattle. I was much more used to a perpetual drizzle than the dry, dusty climate. But home didn't have to be a place. It was people, and my people were *here*.

We pulled into the parking lot of LBK Studios. Campbell reached into the trunk and pulled out his Fender. I held the door for him and stepped inside. We'd worked here on the first and last song we recorded for the new album. It was cozy compared to the behemoth of the studios in LA. Made me feel like coming home.

"I'll take the back booth," I told him. "I like that piano the best."

"Sounds good."

But when I headed toward the back booth, voices made my feet slow. Campbell grinned at me and kept walking.

"Are you expecting anyone else?" I asked.

"Something like that."

I warily followed behind him. What was going on? Why did I feel like I was walking into a carefully laid trap?

"You made it!" Santi's voice boomed before I even turned the corner.

I furrowed my brow and hurried forward to see the entire band sitting in the sound booth, beaming at me. Campbell had just clapped hands with Santi. Viv's hair was now a vibrant hot pink, and her nails were crazy long and mint green. I had no idea how she strummed a bass with them. Yorke was the same as always—taciturn and silent. He tipped his head at me.

"What's going on?"

Campbell grinned back at me. "We talked to Bobby."

Worry bloomed in me. Bobby Rogers...who didn't like me and felt like I had too much influence over the band. But then why was the entire band here? Couldn't they have fired me over the phone or something?

"I see."

"We don't think you do," Viv said, popping her bubblegum.

"We want you to join the band," Campbell said.

Silence. There was silence in my brain. The words I'd

wanted most in the world and convinced myself that I would never hear.

"What?" I managed to get out.

"Yeah, we want you to join," Santi said, clapping me on the back.

"But...Bobby hates me. I thought he would convince you not to make any big changes. This is a big change."

"Bobby doesn't hate you," Campbell burst out at the same time Viv said, "Are you trying to talk us out of it?"

"Yes, he does," I said and then quickly, "No, I'm not."

"It was Bobby's idea," Campbell said.

"What?"

"Well, all of our ideas," Viv said, elbowing Campbell. "We'd been talking about it for a while."

"Yeah, man," Santi said. "We'd discussed it while putting the album together."

"We almost said something in New York," Viv added.

"But we wanted to make sure we could get the contracts and paperwork sorted," Campbell said.

My mouth was open. I stared at the four of them. "You're serious?"

"Yes," Yorke said.

Which sealed it for me. Yorke's word was law.

"Unless you're not interested," Campbell said with a smirk on his lips.

Shithead. He knew I was interested.

"Of course I'm fucking interested."

Campbell laughed and pulled me into a rough hug. "That's what I fucking thought. Welcome to the band."

Viv threw her arms around the both of us, and then Santi joined in.

"Come on, Yorke," Santi coaxed.

Yorke heaved a large sigh and then put one arm around the lot of us. As if it greatly suffered him to be involved in all of this.

We laughed and broke apart, giddy with excitement. The future was suddenly spread out before me. I was joining Cosmere. The biggest band in the world. And not as a roadie, playing my keys in the background, but as one of *them*. How was this my life?

"What do we do from here?" I asked.

"Well, we're heading back to LA tomorrow to get you to sign the paperwork and shit," Campbell said. "We can have it emailed to you to look over...have a lawyer look over."

A lawyer. Right. I needed one of those.

"We can recommend one," Viv said, seeing my deer-in-headlights stare.

"All right." Then, I blinked. "Wait, tomorrow? You just got back."

"Yeah. I know it's short notice. But we want to get everything signed straightaway, and then Bobby wants to run a press announcement about you joining. We'll do a few interviews next week. They were all planned and ready to go as long as you said yes."

"Wow. That's..."

My eyes were wide, and I couldn't even believe it. This was really happening. Finally happening. My big break. My once-in-a-lifetime break. And I was going with them tomorrow.

"He's speechless," Santi said with a laugh. "*Perfecto*. Let's go get a drink to celebrate."

"As long as you're good with all of this," Campbell added.

"Why wouldn't he be good with this?" Santi asked.

Which was the question. Of course this was what I wanted. It was everything I wanted. But now...I knew I had one thing I had to do before I could leave. I was going to have to tell Nora.

My stomach dropped. Things had...escalated between us. We'd started as a fling for her to get over August. We'd agreed to do this until I left. But now, I was leaving. We'd always known that was going to happen, but I thought I had more time. What the fuck was I going to say to her?

Fuck, I needed to figure it out. Because she'd get out of her wedding in a matter of hours, and I'd have to tell her.

"West?" Campbell asked.

"Yeah. Yes. I'm totally cool with it," I said. "Just going to have a lot of people to tell before I go."

"Well, invite everyone out for drinks tonight to say your good-byes," Campbell said. "Because tomorrow, you become a rockstar."

PART V

DREAM JOB

26

NORA

I stifled a yawn.

The Locke-King wedding had been my biggest wedding of the year. Even bigger than Morgan Wright's wedding last year. The Lockes were a wealthy New York City–based powerhouse, and the Kings were one-half of an oil conglomerate. Together, it was the equivalent of marrying a Spanish princess to the King of England.

We'd booked out the entire weekend for this wedding, and Tessi had come with me to shoulder some of the burden. And it was even more beautiful and exhausting than I'd figured.

I watched from the sidelines as Merritt Locke took Margaret King's hand and strode down the aisle of sparklers, arranged perfectly by their guests. They looked happy. Though I was confused by the marriage. They didn't act like besotted lovers. It seemed more...arranged. But they sure knew how to fake it for the cameras. Not that I'd voice any of that out loud. They'd paid me, and that was all that mattered.

Merritt hoisted Margaret's lithe frame up into his enormous arms. I tilted my head slightly to the side, wondering what the Olympic archer's arms *really* looked like underneath that suit.

Tessi nudged me and giggled. "He's *huge*," she whispered.

I shushed her and pretended I hadn't been ogling him. Then, they drove away in an old-timey car. Margaret waved like a princess as she was taken away.

"And that's the exit, boss," Tessi said with a bright smile.

I watched until the car disappeared on the horizon. The magic had left, and now, it was herding cats out of the venue and cleanup. I pinched the bridge of my nose. At least it had gone off without a hitch.

"Need some Tylenol?"

"No. I'm okay. Thanks, Tessi. Could you speak to the DJ?"

She nodded. "On it."

I couldn't hold back my next yawn. I needed some coffee or something to survive the rest of this night. Why hadn't I gotten a hotel room in Midland?

Oh, right. Because I had my own handsome man to get home to. I'd rather spend one more night in his arms than alone in a hotel room.

I pulled out my phone to give West an ETA but found I already had a text from him.

Campbell came back today. We're going to Flips. Join us when you get into town.

I blinked. He wanted me to come out after I got back from Midland? I'd left Lubbock at five thirty in the morning. I wouldn't get back until nearly midnight. The last thing I wanted was to go out and pretend I didn't want to kiss his face off in front of my brother.

It's going to be late.

That's fine. We'll be here.

I groaned. Great. Well, I guess I'd go for one drink and then make an excuse to get away.

I'd just put my phone away when I heard my name called.

"Nora!"

And to my surprise, Gavin King strode toward me. I'd seen him in the midst of his family earlier but not wanted to interfere. Wedding planners weren't seen unless things got out of hand. My goal was to be invisible for nearly everything.

"Gavin, hi," I said with a smile.

His burnished hair was gelled to perfection and his green eyes wide with mischief. There was something in the water here in Midland to create an entire brood of King men this gorgeous.

"How can I help you?"

"Help me?" Gavin asked with a laugh. "Nah, you helped enough."

I arched an eyebrow. "How so?"

"You helped with my date."

"I did?"

I'd seen the blonde on his arm. She was stunning with lush, shoulder-length waves and a liquid-blue silk dress that made me green with envy. She must have been a New Yorker because she seemed to come from another world.

"I invited Whitley," he explained, casually pointing the blonde out again.

I did a double take. "Wait, that's the lavender-haired girl I saw when I was in town?"

"Yeah."

"And you two are..."

He shrugged. "Nah. She's stubborn as hell, and we have...history." He deflated slightly at that, but his eyes were keen when they looked at the beautiful woman who fit in perfectly with his gregarious family. "But keep your fingers crossed for me."

"I'll do just that," I told him.

He winked at me. "Good to see you again."

"You too."

He tipped his head at me and then went after the blonde. I hoped that worked out for him. He didn't seem like the kind of guy who gave up easily. I liked that about him.

It was an hour and a half later before all the guests left and the venue was tidied up to my satisfaction. Tessi had driven into town with me, and we got into my SUV and headed north to Lubbock. We were both too exhausted to even speak much. I dropped her off at her house, and instead of going straight home like I wanted to, I headed drowsily toward Flips.

I hadn't been there since my first lesson with West. That felt like a lifetime ago.

Still, I was surprised they'd picked this for the band. It wasn't exactly under the radar. Not by any stretch of the imagination.

To my horror, I realized precisely why they'd picked it when I stepped inside. It was *karaoke* night.

"What is happening?" I whispered.

My brother—my *rockstar* brother—was onstage, singing a rendition of "Pour Some Sugar on Me" with Viv and Santi.

Yorke stood off to the side with West. Both looked disturbed by the display. Not because they were bad. No, they were excellent. Campbell had a killer voice. Viv and Santi were both good, too. Though not quite as smooth and dreamy. But it was the ridiculousness of the entire situation.

Within the hour, this would be all over social media. Flips would have a surge in patrons, hoping to catch rockstars making fools of themselves more often.

I barreled through the crowd to West's side. I nudged him. "What the hell is going on?"

I could tell at once that he was a little drunk. Not falling-over drunk, but they'd clearly been here for hours.

"Nora!" he cried, sliding his arms around my waist.

I sure hoped that Campbell wasn't paying attention. I hastily pulled out of his grasp. Despite the butterflies going off in my stomach.

"Why are you doing karaoke?"

He shrugged. "Can you contain Campbell?"

No. No one could. Except maybe Blaire, who I noticed was on the other side of the stage with Hollin and Piper. They were all laughing. I waved at them. Hollin waved back. Blaire pointed at Campbell and cackled. Oh, she was enjoying this. Well, good for them.

"It's late," I said around a yawn. "I've had, like, a seventeen-hour day. I'm going to bow out of...whatever this is."

"Wait, wait, wait," West said quickly. "I asked you here for a reason."

"And that is?"

"I was invited to join the band."

The butterflies' wings snapped off and plummeted to their death in my stomach. Everything crashed to a halt. The music drowned out my own thoughts. This was...it was really happening.

Despite my own distress, I knew that I had to be happy for him. No. I *was* happy for him. I wanted him to have the band. I wanted him to have all his dreams come true. This was the best thing that had ever happened to him.

So, I threw my arms around his neck. "Oh my God, West!"

"I know. I know," he gushed. He put me back on my feet and stared down at me. So much unsaid in that look. "We're leaving tomorrow."

"T-tomorrow," I gasped. "Like, in the morning?"

"Early afternoon."

My stomach took a nosedive. Fuck. Fuck, fuck, fuck. I had to tell him. I couldn't hold this in forever. He needed to have all the information before he left. As much as I wanted to contain all of it, I knew that I couldn't. It wasn't fair. None of this was fair.

I wanted to cry.

But I couldn't.

Not here, surrounded by all our friends, when he was alight with excitement.

"That's incredible, West. This is everything you've ever wanted."

He opened his mouth and then closed it. Finally, he nodded. "Yeah, a dream come true."

I wanted to run away and not have to face this. I wanted to wake up from this nightmare. I'd known he was going back to LA. We'd agreed from the start, but it had changed. It had all changed. I didn't know how to be okay with this anymore. I didn't know how to fake it. But fake it was exactly what I had to do.

"Stay for one drink," he pleaded. "I know you're dead on your feet, but we can go home afterward."

"Sure."

I had a drink. I said hi to my brothers. I pretended that everything was okay.

The entire time, my brain spiraled and spiraled. It tried to find the right way to say this. The right way to approach this. But as soon as I came up with something, I discarded it entirely. There was no right way.

It would be better for him to leave and never know. Cleaner. Simpler.

And a lie.

I couldn't lie to him.

We could lie to everyone else, but I refused to do it with him.

So, I finished my drink. I got West to my car and drove us home. He was in a deliriously upbeat mood. I couldn't quite match it, but I was so tired. The alcohol had done nothing but bring me down.

As soon as we stepped inside, I kicked off the shoes I'd had on all day. Even for someone used to heels, my feet hurt. I sighed in relief, and then there was West, picking me up and carrying me to the couch. He sat down and massaged my aching feet.

I nearly burst into tears right there. I loved this man. There was literally no denying it. I loved him, and he was leaving.

"West," I choked out.

He looked up at me, realizing that everything had just gotten very serious. He came to his feet and ran a hand back through his hair, making the longer strands flop back into his face. "We should talk."

"We should."

"You can go first."

"Okay," I whispered. I looked down at my hands, took a deep breath, and then uttered the words I'd wanted to say for so long. "West, I've fallen in love with you."

He stood stock-still. He didn't say anything. He just stared at me.

I couldn't sit under that gaze any longer. It didn't matter that he was still a foot taller than me. I felt like a kid while sitting. I hastily got to my feet and crossed my arms over my chest.

"Say something," I ordered him.

"What do you want me to say?"

I laughed hoarsely. "I don't know. Anything."

"I'm leaving tomorrow."

I took a step backward and swallowed. "I know."

"You knew this was happening."

"We knew you were going back to LA, but not when. Not so soon. It could have been in August. We could have had more time."

"But that's not what happened," he said forcefully.

"I know it's not," I gasped. "You got the dream. You got what you wanted. But...what does that mean for us?"

He paced away from me and back. "I don't know, Nora."

"Because I can't pretend that the last couple of months didn't happen. I can't lie and say that I don't feel anything for you. I do. And I think you do, too."

His jaw set. He wouldn't admit it. He felt it. It couldn't be possible for us to have gone through the exact same experience and not come out feeling the same on the other side of it. This whole thing had been real.

"Say it, West," I demanded. "Say something."

"What should I say that would make any of this easier?"

"Tell me the truth." Tears came to my eyes. Fuck, why did I cry so easily? I could feel him slipping through my fingers, and there was nothing I could do about it. "Tell me you feel something."

"I feel something," he admitted roughly. "Of course I feel something. Is that what you wanted? It doesn't make it any easier."

"We can figure something out."

"How?" he asked. "How can we fix it? You're here. I'm going to be there."

"Blaire and Campbell..."

West choked on a laugh. "Campbell is the biggest rockstar in the world, and Blaire has a job that she can do anywhere. Even for them, with nine years of love between them and a marriage, she's still moving to LA with him because the long-distance is too hard."

My eyes widened. "Blaire is moving there?"

"Not permanently, but yes." His eyes were pleading with me. "Would you come to LA with me?"

I felt so young and stupid in that moment. "What would I do in LA, West?"

"You could work with an event planning firm in the city."

"Do you know how competitive it is to get that kind of work there? Work that's as good as what I'm doing here? I can't go to LA on a hope that I'll find a better job than the one I have here. On top of that, all my friends and family are here, too, except Campbell, who made his choice, and you, who is making the same choice."

My words landed like a jab to the kidney.

West winced. He knew exactly what I'd gone through when Campbell first left. How broken I'd been after the death of our mother and then Campbell just up and leaving me all alone. I'd never quite gotten over my abandonment issues, and it didn't look like it would be happening anytime soon.

"So, you'll stay here, and I'll go there. Just like we planned."

"Neither of us planned this," I shot back.

"The deal was that we would try this until I went back to LA." His eyes hardened, as sharp as daggers. "You said I made my choice. So, I made it. You can't expect me to give up a once-in-a-lifetime opportunity."

"Of course not. I would never tell you to give up the band."

"There's no compromise here," he said. "Neither of us will bend. You won't leave, and I can't stay. Not for you. Not for anyone."

My heart crunched like broken glass being stepped on.

Why had I thought we could work this out? Why had I thought that love would be enough? When in my life had love *ever* been enough?

I'd loved my mom with all of my heart, and still, she'd chosen Campbell over the rest of our family. I'd loved Campbell, and he'd chosen LA. I'd loved August, and he'd chosen Tamara.

It tracked that when I fell in love again, I'd have my heart ripped out of my still-beating chest. Every person I'd ever held on to picked someone else over me. I'd thought that I was moving on from it. West had shown me how to move on, but he was a new source of the same problem.

I wasn't enough.

I'd never ever been enough.

I took a step back as the realization slammed into me like a high-speed train.

"I can't do this," I said and brushed past him and toward my bedroom.

"Nora, what are you doing?"

"Leaving."

"What?" he asked in shock. "Where are you going?"

"I don't know. To Hollin's." Then, I shook my head. "No, my dad's. I can't stay here."

"I'm leaving tomorrow."

"Then, you can spend your last night alone," I said with a shake of my head. "Go live your big dream. I can't be here and love you. Everything about this place is you. It's all you."

"Nora..."

"You made your choice, West." I whipped around to face him. "Tell me you love me. Tell me we can work this out."

I waited. I hoped. I prayed.

But West stared at me and remained silent. Those words didn't pass his lips. He wasn't going to try with me. It wasn't worth it for him.

I'd settled for less than I deserved once before. I wouldn't do it again. So, I turned my back on his silence and packed my suitcase. I held the tears back long enough to get into the car, but then they unleashed until I couldn't even see the windshield. I pulled over and let all the devastation loose.

27

WESTON

I couldn't sleep.

Nora's words rang through my mind. I'd totally fucked it up. Utterly and completely. There was nothing I could say to fix it. I couldn't tell her I loved her. She wouldn't go, and I couldn't stay. Long-distance was never going to work. There was no compromise here. There was only the end, like we'd planned from the start.

After tossing and turning all night, I packed my suitcases, picking my closet clean. Without Nora here, I'd have to figure out what to do with the place. Whitt would probably look over it until I could decide.

Two knocks came from the front door, and then it opened.

"Knock, knock," Whitt said.

I'd asked him this morning if he'd drive me to the airport. He'd texted back, asking why Nora wasn't doing it. I hadn't been able to tell him the truth and just said she was busy.

"Wow, you look like shit," Whitt said with a laugh. "Too much partying last night?"

I ran a hand along the back of my head. "Nora and I... fuck, I don't know what you'd call it. We got into a huge fight, and she left."

"She left the house?" He arched an eyebrow.

I nodded. "I guess we broke up."

Whitt crossed his arms, but he didn't look surprised. "Because you're leaving?"

"Yeah."

"Hmm," Whitt said. He reached for one of my suit-cases. "All right."

"What does that mean?"

"Don't you usually know?"

Yeah, he was right. I sighed. "You think it's for the better."

"Isn't that why you did it?"

I ran my hands down my face. "I don't even know anymore."

Whitt put a hand on my shoulder. "Look, I like Nora. I like you *with* Nora. You seemed steady. She seemed happy. But how would it even work? You're going to be a thousand miles away. And then on tour for most of the year. That's not even possible."

"That's what I said to her."

Still, it felt like every inhalation was glass in my lungs.

Whitt patted me twice. "You know it was the right thing to do."

I followed him out to his car with the other suitcase. We loaded them up and headed back inside for the rest of my stuff and a stiff cup of coffee. Once we got in the car, I felt pulled toward Nora. She was at her dad's. She was probably so pissed at me. Fuck. I hated leaving things like this.

"I feel like I should still talk to her one more time," I told Whitt. "She was so angry when she left."

"Oh no, you don't. That is a bad idea."

"What? Why?"

Whitt shot me an incredulous look. "Do you really not know? You just broke up with her."

"I know, but not because I don't care."

"Does that change anything? Are you going to take her back?"

"No," I told him.

"No. So, what will your presence do?"

I slumped in my seat. "Nothing. It'll hurt her worse."

"Exactly. You're making the right choice. It doesn't feel good right now, but wait until you're in LA, playing with the band. This is what you wanted. What you struggled for. It'll get better."

He was right. I knew he was right. And still, it didn't make me feel any better. I didn't deserve to feel any better. We'd agreed that this was what we'd do. We'd *agreed*. And I'd been the idiot for thinking that would matter.

We arrived in the studio in LA to fanfare. Bobby shook my hand relentlessly. The contracts had been emailed to me last night. Though Viv had offered her attorney's info,

I felt better having someone unrelated to the band look into it.

So, I'd called my dad...

As much as I'd wanted to avoid him at all costs, he had the contacts I needed. He'd readily agreed to have his attorney take a look at it. And by the time I'd landed in LA, I had revised contracts in hand. That simple.

Sometimes, I forgot exactly how much power Owen Wright had. He didn't run Wright Construction anymore, but he sat on the board of directors for other corporations in Seattle now. And the man still knew how to properly throw his weight around.

Bobby and the studio agreed to the revisions, and then I signed the new paperwork. I was officially a member of Cosmere.

"Whoa," I whispered as soon as the papers were signed.

The band congratulated me, and pictures were taken. Blaire stood off to the side with a wide smile on her face. She'd noticed that something was off with me, but I'd avoided her, so I didn't have to have that conversation.

We were immediately whisked to an interview to talk about me joining, then an actual photoshoot, and then a marketing meeting.

By Friday, when we were slated into *Jimmy Kimmel*, I'd barely had a moment to myself, except when I was sleeping. Well, when I should have been sleeping but instead tossed and turned all night. When I managed to drift off, I would wake, feeling like I'd been on an airplane the whole time, jet-lagged and exhausted.

"We're overworking you," Campbell said with a laugh.

I jerked awake in the car on the way to the talk-show set. "Fuck, sorry, dude."

"Too much excitement?"

"Something like that."

"It'll calm down until the album comes out, and then we'll be go, go, go for the next year. Press tours are exhausting, but there's nothing like a world tour. You already know all about that though."

"I'm not sure you'd say my experience as a part of a backup band would be comparable to your world tour."

Campbell shrugged. "You'll do fine. Just need to get some sleep."

"Yeah. Sure. Sleep."

I couldn't tell Campbell the reason I wasn't sleeping. I'd made my choice. He wouldn't exactly be pleased to hear that I'd hurt his sister after all. Not when I'd promised I wouldn't go anywhere near her...and, well, that was too little, too late.

The worst was that I missed her. I wanted her here with me in LA, living through the best moments of my life. Every single one of them would have been better with her here, as she had been in New York City. But that wasn't possible.

We arrived at the set and were taken upstairs to a dressing room. Someone did hair and makeup, much to my chagrin. Apparently, those bags under my eyes were more noticeable than I'd thought.

Then, it was nearly time for our interview when an assistant poked her head inside. "Visitor for Weston Wright."

I blinked in confusion. Who the hell even knew that I

was here? I had some friends in LA that I knew from touring. We'd met up a couple times when I was here for six months to record the album, but none of us were close enough for this. Also, none of them could get backstage at *Jimmy Kimmel*.

I got to my feet and followed the assistant out of the dressing room. And there, standing backstage, as if it were the most normal thing in the world, was Owen Wright.

"Dad?" I asked in confusion. "What are you doing here? *How* are you here?"

"It's good to see you, West."

My dad wrapped an arm around me and pulled me into a hug. I was too shocked to protest. I couldn't figure out what he was doing here. What was the angle? Yes, he knew I was part of Cosmere now. He'd helped with the paperwork after all. But he hadn't told me he was going to be in LA. He hadn't told me he'd be here.

"I don't understand."

"I had business in town. I wanted to surprise you," he said with an easy, charming smile on his face. The smile he always used to get what he wanted.

"I'm surprised," I said stiffly.

He laughed. "Don't be upset. I'm proud of you. I wanted to see you perform. How could I miss this big of an interview when I'm in town?"

"I can't believe they let you backstage."

"I have connections when I need to use them. Do you not want me here?"

"I do," I admitted reluctantly.

As conflicted as I was about my father, I didn't want to

send him away. He was here for *me*. Just me. He'd always gotten along better with Whitt in some ways because they both were in business. As much as he'd tried to understand me, we were too different. It was what had gotten me to go to Lubbock to find out the truth when Whitton could have continued to be blinded by what was happening.

But despite his deceptions, he was still my father. He might have a catch for what he was doing here. It might be as simple as to curry favor now that I was valuable. I still couldn't hate that he was here. Not when I needed the reassurance.

"I can't wait to see you out there. I'm so proud of you, son."

"Thanks, Dad."

My dad was too intuitive though. He tilted his head and assessed me for the first time. Now that I hadn't immediately sent him away. "You don't seem as happy as I thought you would be. Shouldn't this be your victory?"

I sighed heavily. "Yeah, it should."

"What's going on? The dream not as good as you imagined?"

"No, that's not it. Cosmere is the best band. I'm so grateful to be here, with them, getting to do what I love."

"But," he said.

"But...I left someone behind."

"In Lubbock?"

I nodded. "There was this girl."

My dad laughed softly. "Isn't there always?"

"Yeah, I guess." I ran a hand back through my hair before remembering that the hair stylist had spent a decent amount of time making it fall into place exactly. I dropped my hand. So much for that. "She knew I was leaving for LA eventually, but things got sort of serious with us. But when I got the job offer, we broke up."

"That's a difficult situation. I'm sorry to hear that." And he legitimately sounded sincere about it.

"I asked her to come with me," I admitted, crossing my arms and looking away, "but her job is in Lubbock. Neither of us would bend."

"Then it wasn't meant to be."

I frowned. I hated hearing that. Nora and I had felt... right. We had felt like I was suddenly coming up for air. Living without her right now was torture. How could *this* be right?

"Someone has to bend in a relationship for it to work," my dad continued. "That's just how it is."

I narrowed my eyes at him. "You never bent in a relationship."

"I bent more than you know."

My anger grew at those words. "You don't get to sound superior here. You ruined all our lives with your obstinate behavior. You had two relationships, two families. You made everyone compromise but you. I don't want to be like you."

My dad's face fell at those words. "You're right."

"What?" I asked in surprise. I'd been expecting an argument.

"It was my own actions that got me here. I should have been honest. Then, I wouldn't be alone...without either of my families." My dad sighed again. "I'm trying to make it right here. I'm trying to bend for the people I care about now. Be there for you and your siblings when I wasn't. I'd do the same for Jordan and Julian if they let me back into their lives."

"Do you think you deserve *another* chance?"

"No," he said simply. "But I want one."

His body sagged in on itself at the admission. It was then that I could see the gray threading deeper through his brown hair. The circles under his eyes. The weight that had rounded out his middle. Signs that things were not as good for him as he always made them seem to be.

It was hard to feel pity for him after all he'd done, but I did. I felt it then.

After a beat of silence, I said, "I'm glad you're here."

"Good. And I'm sorry about your girl back home. I don't know if it helps, but I think you made the right decision."

It didn't. It really didn't.

But it was the decision that I'd made. I couldn't change anything about it. I just had to live with it. And learn to live without her.

28

NORA

"I'm going to get Hollin over to talk to you, Nora," my dad said, following me around the house.

I grabbed my heels. I needed to go back to West's house to get more clothes. I'd been too exhausted and emotional to pay attention to what I was stuffing into my suitcase. I needed more work clothes. And I needed to get out of my dad's house.

"Don't you dare," I snapped, whirling on him.

"Well, you aren't listening to me."

"I'm not ready to talk about it. I'm not ready to deal with *anything*," I told him. I waved at my face. "Please, I can't cry before I go to work. I don't have time to redo my makeup."

My dad deflated. He absentmindedly rapped his cane against the baseboard. "I'm worried about you. You show up at home in the middle of the night, sobbing. I need to know how to help."

"You can't help, Dad. I wish you could. I wish anyone

could. But I promise that Hollin would only make it worse."

"I can't see how."

Yeah, that was because he didn't know what it was like to have overprotective brothers. Hollin would blow a gasket. He'd fly to LA and put his fist through Weston's face himself. Or worse, call Campbell and have him do it. I didn't want that to happen to West. I loved him too much to ruin his big break.

He'd been on *Jimmy Kimmel* on Friday night. I'd watched with my dad and even managed to keep it together until the interview was over. To pretend to be excited to see Cosmere on TV. West was getting everything he wanted. Good for him.

"I love you, Dad." I kissed him back. "I'll see you after work."

"Love you, too. But how long are you planning to stay?"

"Trying to get rid of me?"

"Of course not. You can stay as long as you want, Nor. I'm concerned."

"I'll start looking for my own place."

"I'm not kicking you out," he said quickly. "I like having you here. I want to help."

But he couldn't.

So, I smiled wanly and headed out to my truck. I was not looking forward to going back to West's for clothes. If I had a friend, I could probably convince them to go with me, but who did I have?

I bit my lip.

Hmm...

I bet I did have someone who would do that with me. I pulled up Eve's number and dialed, connecting it to the Bluetooth in my truck.

"Hey," Eve said. "What's going on?"

"What are you doing tonight?"

"I have to show three houses and walk a couple through closing," she said. "Why? Are you asking me out?"

I choked. "Uh, not exactly. I was wondering if you could help me with something."

"Something that isn't a date?" Eve teased.

"More like detoxing from a man."

"Oh, count me in. What are we doing? Burning sage? Arranging crystals? Calling a demon?"

"Um, wow. That escalated quickly."

"I've done this a time or two before."

I giggled, and it felt good. "You've frequently called a demon?"

"Don't knock it till you try it."

"I'll take your word for it. But, no, I need to get clothes from West's place, but I don't want to go in alone."

Eve sighed softly. "I heard that he went back to LA. He dump you?"

"Pretty much."

"And he kicked you out of his place? What a dick. I mean, Arnold Sinclair had me *evicted*. So, what do I know about men? But damn."

"No, he didn't kick me out," I told her as I pulled into the vineyard. "But I can't stay there, you know?"

"I got you, girl. I'll make time in between my appointments. Text me when you're heading that way. I'll make it work."

"Thanks, Eve," I said truthfully.

I hung up, parked the truck, and headed to my office. I pulled up the long list of things I needed to take care of before the wedding this weekend at the vineyard. Luckily, I didn't have another out-of-town wedding until July. It was truthfully the only one that I was looking forward to. I liked helping my friends here in town, but the rest was a lot of red tape and trying to keep bridezillas from not ruining their big day.

Hollin popped his head in an hour later. "Hey."

I glanced up at him and frowned when I saw the worried expression on his face. "Dad talk to you?"

He strode in and flopped into the chair in front of my desk. "Well, he said you were living with him."

I sighed and closed my eyes. "I told him not to talk to you."

"You going to tell me what's going on?"

"No, I'm not," I growled. "Just leave me alone."

Hollin reared back at my tone. "Nora, it's *me*. When have I ever not been there for you?"

"Hollin, please. I just...I can't talk about it." At the thought of West leaving for LA, tears came to my eyes again, and I blinked furiously to stop them.

"Fuck, you look like someone broke up with you."

I froze at those words.

Hollin noticed though. Of course he noticed.

"This is about West, isn't it?" he asked carefully.

I put my head in my hands. "Do you always have to pry, Hollin? Can't you let me be sad?"

"Nora..."

"Yes, it's about West. And if you tell Campbell that anything happened, I will have your balls," I snapped at my brother, rising to my feet and staring down at him.

Hollin's eyes rounded in shock. I'd never talked to him like this. Not ever.

"Wow. What did he do to you?" he asked, all soft with concern. As if he were approaching a baby deer.

"We were dating, but I didn't want either of you to know. He left for LA. That's what happened. Campbell would go ballistic if he found out. I don't want to break up the band. Swear you won't tell, Hollin."

He nodded slowly. "Okay, okay. I won't tell Campbell. Breathe."

I sank back into my seat. "Thank you. I'm sorry."

"Hey, don't apologize. And don't cry," he said hastily as a tear streaked down my cheek.

"Damn it, Hollin!" I said, reaching for a tissue.

He laughed at that. "What are siblings for?"

"To be a royal pain in the ass."

He snorted. "True story."

I blew my nose. "Thanks."

"Anytime. You know you can come to me. Even though I want to punch him."

"And that's why I didn't."

"I would have listened. I don't want you to think that I wouldn't."

"You punched August."

"He was making out with Tamara!" he cried. "That is not the same story. Then, they got engaged. He fucking deserved it."

"Yeah, well, they're not engaged anymore. Tamara called to tell me that he dumped her because he was still in love with me."

"Tell me you're not going to go back to him. I'll punch him again for emphasis."

"No, that's long over. He started texting after it happened. I told him I wasn't interested and to leave me out of the drama."

"That's grown-up of you."

I sighed. "I don't know. I can't deal with anyone else's problems when I'm going through my own heartbreak."

"I understand that perfectly. Just...try to keep your chin up," he said gently as he came to his feet. "You're perfect just the way you are. If Weston Wright didn't see that, then he doesn't deserve you."

Tears spilled onto my cheeks again. "Thanks, Hollin."

Then, he disappeared, back to work. I stared down at the mound of paperwork in dismay. Fuck, I needed to stop crying every time I thought about West. It wasn't like he was coming back.

I met Eve at West's house after work. She rubbed her hands together.

"Let's do the damn thing," she said.

"You're enthusiastic."

Eve put an arm around my shoulders. "No. I'm sorry about everything that happened. I feel partially responsible since I set you on this path. We agreed that, of course, you wouldn't have to end up together, but I didn't plan for what would happen if you did fall for him and he left."

"That's not on you. I didn't really think it through either."

"All right. Let's go empty your closet. I brought my secret weapon." She held up a box of garbage bags.

"Trash bags?"

"You can't pack a closet without them. Realtor secret. Come on."

I shook my head and followed her into the house. It was exactly as I'd left it. I'd neglected the plants, and I nearly started crying again when I found one of my babies wilting. I let Eve into my bedroom as I took a watering can around to all the plants. I'd have to figure out what to do with them all. I couldn't bring a proper garden into my dad's house. And I didn't have a new place yet to move them. Which meant I needed to come over more frequently to take care of them.

I sighed. Just one more thing.

"Oh my God, your shoes!" Eve shrieked from the bedroom.

I laughed at her assessment. "Pretty amazing, right?"

"A girl's dream. You want all of them?"

"Yeah. Let's just clear everything out."

I grabbed another garbage bag when my phone began to ring. I glanced down at the number, but I didn't recognize the area code. Half of my job was answering strange phone calls from people about weddings. The number of people without an 806 area code in Lubbock was sometimes dizzying.

"I'm going to take this," I told Eve, holding up the

phone. She waved me off, and I answered it. "Hello, Nora Abbey speaking."

"Nora, hi, it's English. Anna English."

My feet stilled in the kitchen. English. Oh my God, she'd called. I took a deep breath to calm my racing heart.

"English, hi. It's so good to hear from you."

"I'm so sorry it took me this long to get back to you. I'll admit, partially, I wanted to see how you'd do with an event as big as the Locke-King wedding. I spoke to Gavin and Whitley. They had nothing but rave reviews of the event. They said it was utterly seamless."

"I'm so pleased to hear that. I've been working in weddings for about five years, and it's where my true passion lies."

"That's what I like to hear. Plus, I hate my wedding planner. It was so nice to fire her this morning."

"How did your mother-in-law take it?"

"Eh," she said with a laugh. "It was fine. I told her it was fire the wedding planner or we elope, and she came around."

I chuckled. "I bet she did."

"So, I'd love to have you on board. You can feel free to send over your contract, or I can share the one that we used with our last planner, which includes a five-thou-sand-dollar retainer."

I nearly sank to the floor at those words. A five-thou-sand-dollar *retainer*. I didn't make that much on most of my weddings, period. The Locke-King wedding had paid well, but not like this. Holy shit.

"That would...that would be great. I would be open to either. Whatever you prefer."

"Excellent. I'm so excited about this. We'll have to arrange a meeting in the city, so we can discuss everything that's in the works. You can meet my mother-in-law."

The mayor of New York City. So casual.

"Thank you for the opportunity."

"No, thanks for saving my ass," she said with a laugh.

We said a few more pleasantries, and then I hung up in a state of shock. Then, I screamed and did a twirl.

Eve came hurtling out of the bathroom with a shoe in her hand. "Is it a spider? I'll kill it!"

I laughed and flopped onto the ground. "I got the job."

"The job?"

"As a celebrity wedding planner."

"Oh my God! Nora!" Eve did a little dance and pulled me up into a hug. "That deserves to be celebrated. Ice cream?"

I nodded. "Ice cream."

And though I was devastatingly happy, the one person I wanted to share the news with was no longer someone I could call. I promised myself it wouldn't ruin the moment, but I'd lied to myself before.

29

WESTON

It wasn't until the initial rush of excitement over officially joining the band began to wear off that everything hit me with the worst bout of depression I'd had in years. I'd managed it with music, growing up, but the only song I wanted to play now was "Nora's Melody."

Even my music had turned against me.

Apparently, I would just suffer for my choice. I'd read *Crime and Punishment* in high school and never understood Dostoevsky's point about how guilt could cause such mental anguish that a person would deteriorate. But I certainly understood now, I couldn't go on like this. I just couldn't.

So, I'd given up on trying to be okay.

I went to the studio. I still felt strange about walking into a booth this fancy with or without the rest of the band. But it felt necessary. I'd been avoiding the song for long enough.

I sat at the piano and began to work out the full tune to "Nora's Melody." It flowed like it had been held captive for weeks. A trickle turning into a stream and then a deluge.

The door creaked open behind me, and my fingers stilled.

"Hey, man."

I found Campbell in the doorway with his hands in his leather jacket and a look of confusion on his face. "You came."

"Cryptic message," he said, entering our sanctum. "After that, how could I not?"

"I need you to do something for me."

Campbell arched an eyebrow. "What's that?"

"Listen to this song."

He toed the door closed behind him and nodded. "All right. What you got?"

Nerves bit into me fresh and raw. I wasn't sure if I was doing the right thing here. But no matter how many people said that I'd made the right choice, I knew it wasn't true. Because it wasn't a choice at all.

It was a theft.

A coward's way out.

And I'd been a lot of things, but never that.

So, I cleared my throat, prepared for everything that would follow by the end of this. All the consequences to my actions. And I sang.

No one had ever told me that I should be a lead singer. It had always irritated me that I could play ten instruments, but my voice would never match the tunes I could play. But I'd fallen so in love with music that I never really cared. And truthfully, it didn't matter for this song that I didn't have Campbell's crooning voice.

The earnestness to the song made up for the rough vocals. I'd been holding it all back for so long that the song erupted out of me. A volcano pouring lava down a mountainside, flowing freely for the first time in ages.

And by the time I let the last note fade away, I felt as if I'd been exorcized.

We were both silent for a minute. My eyes closed as I held the sustain pedal down to let the last notes linger in the air. A mourning quality to the piece that had never been there before I royally fucked up.

The note finally ended, and I opened my eyes to find Campbell thoughtfully staring at me. My cheeks reddened, and I removed my hands from the piano. "What do you think?"

"You're a little pitchy," Campbell said with a smirk.

I snorted. "More than a little."

Campbell held his hands up. "I wasn't going to say it."

I stared down at the keys and released the tension in my shoulders. "I wrote it about your sister."

"Ah," he said softly.

"Ah?" I asked, jerking my head back up to look at him. "That's it? You're not going to punch me?"

Campbell shrugged. "I could if you'd like me to?"

"Uh, no. No, thanks. I just...I don't understand."

"Well, I'm not stupid."

I blinked at him. "You knew that Nora and I were together?"

"I had my suspicions. You're not exactly sneaky. Did you think you were being sneaky?"

"Uh...yeah," I said slowly. "I thought you were going

to kill me. You said to my face that you'd kill anyone who touched her."

"Oh, I know," he said, dropping into a chair across from me. "I had every intention of doing just that. I was even halfway to your house one night when Blaire helped to talk me down."

"Blaire knows, too?" I ran a hand back through my hair. "Jesus, does everyone know?"

"Hollin doesn't know or else you would have a black eye."

I grimaced. "Yeah. So, uh, you're taking this better than I thought. What the hell did Blaire say to you to get you not to beat the shit out of me?"

"She reminded me that I liked and trusted you. That we were friends for a reason. And if I respected you as much as I did—" He shot me a look. "Which I do. I wouldn't have asked you to join the band if I didn't think you were worth the shot." He rubbed his hands together. "Then I should respect you enough to take care of my sister as well."

"And you listened to her?" I asked in shock.

He chuckled. "Uh, no. She was right, of course. But I wouldn't hear a fucking thing about it. I wanted to make you pay." He met my gaze and shrugged. "It was Nora actually."

"Wait, Nora told you?" I asked, coming to my feet. "There's no way. She would have mentioned—"

He held his hand up. "She didn't tell me. It wasn't like that."

I sat back down. "Oh."

"But it was still Nora who convinced me. You remember after she and August broke up?"

I nodded. I hated thinking of her that way, but, yeah, I couldn't ever forget how she'd been a broken, empty vessel. Sand poured out of an hourglass.

"Well, that wasn't the first time I'd seen her like that. She was like that after Mom died. And she dragged herself out of it after a lot of time, but I wasn't there to help her like I should have been. I didn't want that to happen again. I promised I'd be there. So, I was pissed, thinking you were taking advantage of her depressive state."

"I would never..."

"I know. Because that night I went to your house, I saw Nora happy. You were sitting in the living room, playing a video game. She would laugh her head off and then pounce on you. You'd lift her off you like she weighed nothing and drop her down on the couch. She'd wiggle away and snatch the controller back to play again. Blaire took one look at me and was like...would you be helping or hurting if you barged in right now?

"And she was right. Nora was happy. She was the happiest I'd ever seen her. I didn't know what was going on between y'all. It wasn't my place to interfere anyway. As long as she was happy, that was what mattered. If you make her happy, that's what I want. That's all I've ever wanted for her."

I nearly choked. I remembered that night. So many nights when we'd dicked around at home. Deliriously happy, away from the rest of the world. In our own little bubble.

And I'd ruined that.

"I just figured you weren't that serious after all," Campbell said.

I hung my head. "We were. I fucked up."

"Should I punch you now?"

"Uh, no," I said quickly. "Not helpful. Mostly, I keep seeing everything as black and white. Her job is in Lubbock. Mine is here. We'd agreed that when I went back to LA, it would be over. I hadn't realized how far we'd come in the time we had."

"Do you love her?" Campbell asked. "Because if you love her, then all that other shit doesn't matter. You'll figure it out."

And somehow, it was all so clear. We'd just figure it out. It had seemed so cut and dry in Lubbock. I still had no clue how it was going to work out. Things were fucking hard as hell, but still, I had to try.

I met his gaze. "Yeah, I do."

Campbell nodded. "Good. That's the right answer."

He held his hand out to me. I clapped mine into his, and he helped me to my feet, pulling me into a hug.

"I have to fix this."

"Yeah, you do because if you leave my sister broken, then I'll actually have to throw that punch."

I laughed. "That seems fair."

"All right, what's the plan?"

And that was when it all materialized before me. I knew exactly what to do. Exactly how to win her heart one more time.

30

NORA

"What the hell is this?" Hollin asked.

I passed him the paperwork. He stared down at it and back up at me. Piper was seated next to him. She craned her neck to look at the paper, and her eyebrows shot up.

"Nora!" Piper said in surprise.

"My two-week notice."

"You're quitting?" Hollin asked in dismay. "What? What for?"

I handed him a second piece of paper. "This is why."

Hollin snatched it out of my hand and stared down at it. His eyes got huge. "Holy shit, Nora!"

"Oh my God, this was what Eve was so excited about the other night!" Piper cried. "She wouldn't tell us until you said so."

"Yeah. Eve was there when I got the call. It's a contract to work for the Kensingtons as a wedding planner for English and Court's wedding."

"A celebrity wedding," Hollin said softly. "That's what you wanted."

I'd accepted the offer from English and signed the contract the next day. This one wedding was two-thirds of my entire salary for the year, working twenty-six weddings or *more* a year. And instead, I could just work with this one. But I'd need to be in New York, and I couldn't do that and keep my job here full-time.

I nodded. "Seemed unlikely to happen when I hadn't been in the industry for longer, but I got lucky when we were in New York. I would be an idiot to turn this down."

"Be happy for her!" Piper said, smacking Hollin on the arm.

He laughed and rose to his feet. He pulled me into a hug. "I'm proud of you."

"Thanks. So, we'll need to bring on another planner. I can shift a lot to Tessi, but I was doing the work of three people—"

"Wait, wait, wait," Hollin said. He held his hand up. "No."

"No, what?"

He took my two-week notice in his hands and tore it in half. My eyes widened, and I gaped at my older brother.

"What the hell are you doing?"

"Hollin!" Piper said.

"You don't have to quit. The office is still yours. You can do as much or as little as you want here. Hell, make your celebrity dreams come true and use the office as headquarters. We have plenty of space."

"What? Seriously?"

"Of course. You're my sister. You can give all the weddings up if you want. We'll hire someone else. We'll bring Tessi up to speed. Whatever you want, but I won't accept this." He held the torn paper back to me.

I looked at him in shock, and Piper just shook her head.

"You could have warned her," Piper said with a sigh. She came to her feet and drew me into a hug. "I'm so happy for you, whether you stay in Lubbock and have your base of operations here or move to New York or whatever you do. Proud of you."

"Me too," Hollin said.

Tears came to my eyes, and finally, they were happy tears. No more crying over boys. No more crying for broken hearts. I didn't know what was in store for me, but at least I was moving in the direction of my dream job. It was worth it, even with only one big wedding booked, to see what I could do out there. To see how far I could take it. Because I had big dreams, too, and there was a whole wide world out there to make them come true.

———

"Okay, should I walk you through it one more time?" I asked.

Tessi looked up at me with a blank expression on her face.

"What?" I asked with a laugh. "It's not as bad as it seems."

"I went from ten weddings this summer to eighteen, Nora. It's terrifying."

"You're not going to do them all on your own. We're bringing someone else on full-time to handle the bulk of the work. She'll take the twelve other weddings that I had on my docket and assist you with the eight larger weddings."

"Right. Right," Tessi said with wide eyes.

"I'm still going to be here," I reminded her. "I have six weddings on my plate."

Just not the twenty-six weddings I'd had on my plate from now until October. Which was absurd anyway now that I looked at it. But it had been my job, and I was the best at it.

"I know," she said on a long exhale. "And I'm happy for you. You deserve it. Just nervous. I was only brought on full-time last month."

"You can do this. I'm always a phone call away, Tes."

I wasn't sure that I'd helped her anxiety about what was happening, but I couldn't fix it all either. I'd stay on for the bigger ones that Tessi needed help with. Lubbock was still home, and it was my brother's winery after all. But I was excited to head to New York and work on bigger and bolder weddings. Making all my dreams come true.

"I'm glad you're not leaving full-time. Because I am not you, Nora Abbey," Tessi said with a laugh.

"You're not me. But you're Tessi, and you're going to do magical things. I believe in you."

Tessi beamed. "Thanks."

A knock sounded at my door, and I looked up to find Hollin standing in the doorway. "Hey, can I borrow you a minute?"

"Sure." I handed Tessi another file. "Look over all this and let me know if you have any questions."

I strode out of the office and followed Hollin through the cellars.

"What's going on? Not reconsidering taking my two-week notice, are you?"

Hollin rolled his eyes. "Definitely not. You're staying as long as you want. If you become big and famous like Campbell, then we'll talk about it again."

I snorted. "No one is as famous as Campbell."

"Good. Then, it's settled."

I rolled my eyes. Typical.

We headed up from the cellars toward the barn. It was a beautiful May afternoon. Not a cloud in the sky. Hardly even any wind, and in Lubbock, that was a feat. It made me want to ride with the windows down and the music blasting. It made me want to live again.

Except none of it was the same since West had left. I was trying to be myself again. It had only been about three weeks. So, I gave myself grace to feel sad. The new job had definitely helped. But it didn't make it all go away. Living without him was harder than it ever should have been.

I still hadn't figured out what to do about the plants. I didn't have my own place, and so I'd gone over every few days to water. Only bringing over the most delicate plants to my dad's house. He'd side-eyed me but let it go. Hollin must have spoken to him because he'd given me my space since then.

Mostly, I just missed West.

I missed having him to come home to every day.

I missed his laugh and the little face he'd made when I was being ridiculous and the way he'd insisted on driving me around.

I missed his hands.

It was crazy to miss someone's hands. But his were perfect. Callous from playing instruments his whole life. Big and strong and careful and caring and adoring.

I sighed as we neared the barn. The world might keep turning, but I was stuck in the past.

"Nora?" Hollin asked.

"Yeah? Sorry. I zoned out."

"It's fine. What were you thinking about?"

My cheeks colored. "Nothing. What were you saying?"

"You know I love you, right?"

I narrowed my eyes. "Yeah. What's going on? Are you up to something?"

He snorted. "So much for me trying to be nice."

"We're siblings. *Nice* isn't the first word I'd use to describe our affection."

"I wasn't being an asshole. Just go inside."

"Why?"

He shook his head and walked away.

"Hollin?" I called after him.

But he didn't turn around. I took one step after him but stopped when I heard music coming from inside the barn.

My stomach dropped, and a hand went to my heart. I turned slowly back to face the barn door. I knew that song. I'd heard it in my house as Weston's fingers moved effortlessly across the keys. I knew it as my own.

But it wasn't possible.

With a gulp, I pulled open the door and stepped inside.

Weston was sitting in front of a piano on the Wright Vineyard stage, singing *my* song.

31

NORA

My hands went to my face as tears came to my eyes.

The tears I'd sworn I'd never cry again.

But that all went out the window with what was in front of me. Weston was here. He was in Lubbock, at the winery, on the stage...for *me*.

His fingers coaxed the piano to life. His vocals came out almost haunted through the microphone. And the melody that had lulled me into love with him wrapped itself around me.

And the rest of the band was there. Santi tapping out a soft drumbeat. Viv adding a low bass beat. Yorke strumming a refrain on his guitar. And my brother, the lead singer and bona fide rockstar, stood in the back with a guitar strapped to him as he sang *backup*. Actual *backup* to West's vocals.

He winked at me when I caught his eye. Had West told him? Had he found out? What was he even doing here if he knew? Shouldn't he be furious? I couldn't comprehend how this had all come to be.

But I could focus on nothing as I stood frozen, listening to West sing about me. I'd never had a song written about me. Definitely not one performed by Cosmere of all things. There was no way this was happening.

Then, just as it had started, the song ended.

And West met my gaze. Regret in every bit of those big blue eyes. He smiled at me. Everything I'd gone through these weeks without him. All the pain I'd endured in his absence. One song couldn't possibly fix it all. And yet something cracked inside of me, and the tears spilled down my cheeks. This was what I'd wanted. It was all I'd wanted.

The rest of the band filed backstage, and Campbell hopped off to meet me. He wrapped his arms around me tight, whispering in my ear, "Just hear him out, shrimp."

I laughed hoarsely. "I thought you'd hate him for this."

"I only ever want the best for you. If he's it, then that's what I want. I'm sorry for ever making you think otherwise."

He kissed my forehead, ruffled my hair—to my dismay—and then followed the rest of the band out of the barn, leaving West and me all alone.

He stood from the piano and dropped down off the stage. "Hey."

"Hey?" I asked through my tears. "Weeks of radio silence, and now, you say *hey*?"

"I missed you," he said, walking carefully toward me.

"You can't miss me."

"I did. Every minute."

"Why are you here? How did you convince Campbell not to kill you?"

"Apparently, he already knew."

I sputtered, "What?"

That didn't make any sense. Not a single ounce of sense. Campbell had made West worry that he wouldn't even be accepted into the band. How had he known and just let it pass?

"I was as surprised as you are."

"Oh, I doubt that," I told him. As happy as I was to see him, I didn't forget the last three weeks of misery that easily.

"I deserve all of your wrath. I do. I can completely understand how you'd be furious with me."

"Good. Because I am."

"But I've been miserable without you, too."

"Good."

He laughed and nodded. "I deserve that. I earned it in fact. I pushed you away and made you think that what I felt, what we both felt, wasn't important. And for that, I'll never forgive myself. I spent the last three weeks in LA, where I was supposed to be living my best life, wanting nothing more than to have you there with me."

I crossed my arms over my chest. I wanted so much to give in to him, but I needed more than an *I'm sorry*. More than an *I deserve that*. It wasn't enough.

"I tried to be happy in LA without you, Snickers, but it wasn't possible. I don't want this life if I can't share it with you."

"You're the one who picked this," I said, my voice cracking.

"I know. And I was wrong. And I'm trying to do everything I can to fix this. I invited Campbell to the studio, and I played him your melody. I told him about us. He laughed and told me he already knew because he wasn't an idiot."

I laughed softly. "That sounds like him."

"He said that when he found out, Blaire came with him to confront us. She said that if he respected me as much as he did, then he should be happy that we were together. Not try to tear us apart. He wasn't planning to listen to her, but you know what changed his mind?"

I shook my head. "What?"

"You did."

I blinked. "Come again?"

"He saw how happy you were. The happiest he'd ever seen you was when you were with me. And he wanted that for you. He wants you to be as happy as you were when he saw you with me."

I sniffled at that. "I was happy."

"And I ruined it."

"Yeah, you did."

He took another step forward until we were nearly touching. "I hate what I did. I was seeing things in only one way. I couldn't find a way to make this work."

"So, how do you know it'll work this time?"

His hand dropped to my chin and lifted my head to look up at him. "Because I love you."

I melted at those words. The words I'd been so desperate to hear for so long. Words I'd never thought I'd hear. Not after how everything ended. Not after he walked out without ever uttering them.

"You do?" I asked, wanting so bad for it to all be true.

"I always have. I loved you when you refused to let me into my own house because you'd redecorated. I loved you when you crawled around on the ground as a delirious drunk. I loved you when you trusted me enough to take care of you. I loved you here, and I loved you in LA. I've always loved you, and I always will."

A tear spilled down my cheek. He swiped his thumb across my cheek to capture the tear.

"I love you, Nora Abbey."

A laugh burst from my chest. "You're back."

"I really am. I'm here for you. I refuse to be separated from you ever again."

"But what about LA?" I asked, looking up into his eyes.

He frowned. "We'll figure it out. I know I said that it wasn't possible before, but I discovered it's impossible to live without you. I'll fly back. We'll video-chat. I'll fly you out. I don't know. As long as you're mine, I don't care. I know how important your job is to you. I know that you belong here. I won't forget it or try to change you. I want you to do what you find most important. I'll be here for the ride."

I sniffled again and threw my arms around him. He had no idea about the job offer. He had no idea how much had changed in the few weeks since he'd been gone.

"I want to go with you," I told him.

He pulled back fiercely and looked alarmed. "What?

No. Nora, you can't give this up for me. That's not okay. I was wrong to even suggest it last time."

"West, no..."

"I'm serious," he said, grasping my hands. "I want you to be happy. I don't want you to have to give up your passion or try to start over in LA."

I laughed and pressed a kiss to his lips. Those were the perfect words. The words I'd needed to hear that he was sincere. He would figure this all out with me if I asked him to.

He drew me against him, wrapping his arms around my waist and kissing me, as if he'd been crumbling to dust without me and I was making him solid again. "I love you, Nora."

"I love you, too," I whispered. "But I'm still coming with you."

He looked alarmed. "You're going to quit your job? But I thought..."

"English offered me the job."

"Oh my God," he said, momentarily stunned. "You're going to be working a celebrity wedding?"

I nodded vigorously. "I start next week. I already put in my two-week notice here. Hollin asked me to stay on and help while we onboard new employees or even run my own company out of the vineyard, but I could do that in LA, too."

"You...quit your job."

"Yes. The fee for that one wedding is most of my salary here. And it'll give me a year to see if this is the right move for me. Maybe even a year in LA to find a new job."

"You're serious." His eyes were wide with shock. "You want to come to LA with me?"

I took a deep breath. "Can we bring the plants?"

He burst into laughter, swinging me in his arms and twirling me in place. "We can bring all the plants. I'll get you as many beautiful plants as you want. Everything and more."

I giggled and clung to him. "You know, in LA, I can grow citrus trees."

"I'll get you a whole grove," he told me.

He set me carefully back onto my high heels and pressed another deep kiss against my lips. The rest of the world disappeared in that embrace. Weston Wright loved me. He'd come back for me. Been willing to make it work while I stayed in Lubbock. I might not have forgiven him any other way, but this was exactly how it always should have been.

So, I put the past behind me and gave myself over to this man.

"I love you, West."

"And I love you, Nora."

We'd started out as roommates, tried it out as a fling, and ended up forever. What more could a girl ask for?

EPILOGUE

THREE YEARS LATER

The enormous trifold mirror in the bridal suite showed me from multiple angles. All revealing the sweeping lace and princess skirt of my wedding dress, the delicate twist to my medium-blonde hair, and the half-dozen bridesmaids I'd chosen for this momentous day. Eve was closing the several dozen buttons along the back of my dress as the rest of the girls oohed and aahed at my appearance.

"You're a vision," Blaire announced.

"Thank you."

Eve grunted. "Whoever invented this many buttons was a masochist."

Annie chuckled and nudged her out of the way. "I know it's a maid-of-honor duty, but if I can sew perfect stitches, I can button her into a dress."

Eve's eyes rounded as Annie made quick work of the buttons. "How?"

"You get used to Annie's incredible competence,"

Piper said, holding up a glass of the new Abbey sparkling vintage.

"I like a girl with deft fingers," Viv said, popping a bubblegum bubble. Her hair was a striking hot pink for the occasion. She'd asked me if I wanted her to dye it a "normal" color, and I'd looked at her as if she were absurd. Three years on tour with Viv, and she had never once had a "normal" hair color. I couldn't imagine her any other way.

Annie winked at her. "If I wasn't already married with a kid, I'd consider that offer."

"Aww, and Rush is so cute," Jennifer said, snapping pictures of the lot of us. She was in a bridesmaid dress, but she wasn't an official bridesmaid. It had been hard enough, narrowing it down to six, but she'd insisted she preferred to be behind the camera anyway.

"The cutest," Blaire agreed.

"I don't know," I said. "June and Oliver are pretty adorable."

Blaire beamed. "They are."

Right before the album release, Blaire and Campbell had gotten pregnant with June, who was almost-three-year-old now. Baby Oliver had followed shortly afterward, and she'd already confessed to me that she was pregnant for a third time. Though it was too new for anyone to see yet. I was hoping for another niece!

"You're just biased because they're your niece and nephew," Piper said.

"Fair."

Jennifer touched her pregnant belly. "I wonder if I'll

have a boy or another girl. Violet wants a sister, but Julian wants a boy."

"I can't believe you don't want to know!" Eve gushed.

She shook her head. "I know it's crazy, but we both want to be surprised. Jordan and Annie know, but we don't."

We all whipped around to look at Annie. She held her hands up. "We're the godparents! It's not my fault. Don't try to get it out of me."

"All this baby talk," Harley said, gagging.

All of us laughed at her. She might be twenty-two and freshly graduated from Texas Tech and on her way to law school, but she was still that little teenager to me. I was glad she wasn't thinking about babies. There was plenty of time left in her life before that.

"Babies are overrated," Piper said, passing Harley a glass of sparkling and dropping down next to her. They hit knuckles.

Piper and Hollin had moved in together, but there were no impending nuptials or babies in their near future. I wasn't surprised, nor did I care, as long as they were happy. That was all that really mattered. And truly, they were happier than I'd ever seen them. Especially with the vineyard breaking monetary goals year after year, and the wine far exceeding expectations.

"Are we almost ready?" Tessi asked, stepping into the bridal suite.

I nodded, smiling at my friend. "All set."

Tears came to Tessi's eyes as she caught sight of me. "Oh my God, Nora. Look at you!"

I did a twirl in my dress, the material swirling in little eddies at my feet as I moved. It was a one-of-a-kind dress. It had been made personally for me by Harmony Cunningham. I'd planned her wedding, and she'd insisted when my time came, she would fit me like a princess. And she had.

Planning English's wedding had changed my life. I'd told myself one year to figure out what I was going to do if I never booked another celebrity wedding. But the day after English's wedding I'd had a dozen weddings lined up for the next year. My salary was through the roof. And every wedding after that brought in more and more incredible offers, that I'd had to hire an assistant to screen who I would work with.

A year later I had my own wedding firm in LA with a half dozen planners working underneath me. Abbey Weddings had taken off like I'd never imagined in my wildest dreams. And with more people working for me, I had all the time I needed to join West on tour while the ship ran itself. But when West had proposed to me at White Sands on a dune all alone, I'd known the only place that I would want to get married was right here at Wright Vineyard.

"Let's go get you married," Tessi said.

My bridesmaids all filed out in front of me. I took one last fortifying sip of the sparkling wine and then followed them to the door.

I'd always dreamed about my wedding. What girl who wanted to become a wedding planner didn't dream of her wedding? But even if I'd imagined it, I'd never thought it would be as big or as beautiful as it was. All of my friends and family from Lubbock were in attendance, of course, but people from all over the country had flown in for the occasion. Couples that I'd worked with who had become friends over the years, our friends from LA, and West's friends from Seattle filled the outdoor space.

"Oh Nora," my father said.

"Dad." I threw myself into his arms. He held me tight.

"You look beautiful. I'm so proud of you."

"I love you so much. Thanks for always being there for me, even when I didn't know what I needed."

"Of course, honey. I know it was hard, growing up without your mom, but I tried my best to be all that you could ever need. Even when I fell short, I was trying."

"You did the best. I am who I am because of you, Dad."

He tapped his cane twice against the wood of the barn. "Wish I could walk you down that aisle without this."

I took his hand and stilled the cane. "That's a part of you. I wouldn't want you any other way."

He beamed at my compliment. "I couldn't have asked for a better daughter."

"Well, that's lucky. Because you only have one."

He laughed. "Come on, sweetheart. Let's get you married."

He held his elbow out, and I looped our arms together.

The bridesmaids went first, standing on the other side of the groomsmen—Whitton, Campbell, Jordan, Julian, Santi, and Yorke. Three years in Cosmere had solidified West's place in the band. He was one of them now. Santi and Yorke were as much his brothers as Whitt, Jordan, and Julian were.

He and Campbell were closer than ever, working on new music together, as they always had here in Lubbock. The fans loved him, and he'd even gotten his own fanbase nickname—Westies. I still laughed, thinking about his face when he'd found out what they were calling themselves.

"You're up," Tessi told me.

The entire audience rose to their feet as "Nora's Melody," played by a string quartet, filled the air. My heart rose to my throat at the first note of that song. It had never become a Cosmere song. Though they'd argued awhile about whether it should go on the next album. But West swore, until the day he died, that the only person that song belonged to was me. And it was forever my song.

My dad took the first step forward across the rose-lined pathway. I held my head high as we moved toward my groom. The rest of the audience became a blur as I walked. I knew my friends and family were there. West's mom and dad sitting on opposite sides of a bench in the front row. My aunts on the opposite side with a space left for my dad. But still, I didn't meet any faces.

Every wedding that I'd ever done, my favorite moment was when the groom caught sight of his bride for the first time. It was magical. This look of pure adoration and disbelief that he'd gotten lucky enough to have this woman. Sometimes, he cried. Sometimes, he had to cover his mouth. Sometimes, he just looked shocked. Every time, it was beautiful. Every single one was the perfect moment for them. I'd never trade it. Not for anything.

And now, I got to have my moment with *my* groom.

I turned down the aisle, and there he was.

Weston Wright.

My groom. My forever.

A smile broke onto his face, a look of pure awe as his gaze ran down my dress and then back up to my face. It was a new look. And yet so like how he'd been looking at me every day for the last three years. This was the magic, the moment. But it came from a million magical moments over the course of our relationship. It came from knowing he loved me as much now as he had that day he came back to Lubbock and tried to make it all right.

We'd jumped that day.

And he'd been catching me every day since.

My dad handed me off to him, and West couldn't even help himself. He brought my hands to his mouth and kissed them.

"You're real."

"I'm real," I whispered back.

"Marry me."

I giggled. "Sort of in the process of that."

The crowd chuckled behind us. We stepped up to the dais before a circular gold archway, covered in pink flowers and greenery. The vineyards were in full bloom behind us. The sun sinking toward the horizon and the world narrowing to just the two of us as we each said our *I do*s, confirming our union.

"I love you," he whispered, thick with emotion.

"I love you, too."

"I now pronounce you husband and wife. You may kiss the bride."

Then, West swept me into his arms, dipping me dramatically. Our lips sealed together.

A promise for tomorrow.

A promise for forever.

A promise that we were eager to fulfill.

West pulled me back to my feet, joined our hands, and held them overhead.

"I present to you Weston and Nora Wright!"

THE END

ACKNOWLEDGMENTS

Thank you to everyone who helped me write this book. Nora & West were so fun to work with. And I couldn't have done it without all the people who worked tirelessly in the background to get to this moment.

The soundtrack to this book was: Taylor Swift's RED album (Taylor's Version), Not Friends by Maisie Peters, and the B side of Olivia Rodrigo's Sour album.

ABOUT THE AUTHOR

 K.A. Linde is the *USA Today* bestselling author of more than thirty novels. She has a Masters degree in political science from the University of Georgia, was the head campaign worker for the 2012 presidential campaign at the University of North Carolina at Chapel Hill, and served as the head coach of the Duke University dance team.

She loves reading fantasy novels, binge-watching Supernatural, traveling to far off destinations, baking insane desserts, and dancing in her spare time.

She currently lives in Lubbock, Texas, with her husband and two super-adorable puppies.

Visit her online:
www.kalinde.com

Or Facebook, Instagram & Tiktok:
@authorkalinde

For exclusive content, free books,
and giveaways every month.
<u>www.kalinde.com/subscribe</u>

CPSIA information can be obtained
at www.ICGtesting.com
Printed in the USA
LVHW100419230622
721876LV00014BB/120